LASTING INFLUENCE

A few clicks away from murder

LINDA HAGAN

THE BOOK FOLKS

Published by The Book Folks

London, 2024

ISBN 978-1-80462-226-1

www.thebookfolks.com

Lasting Influence is the eighth novel in a series of standalone murder mysteries set in Belfast and beyond.

Chapter 1

The elderly man was on his knees in the centre of the room. He was shaking. His hands were held together as if in supplication but he wasn't praying. At least not to the god he had never believed in before tonight.

All around him the room was in chaos. Books, papers, files were strewn carelessly over the floor. A chair was overturned in the corner. A lamp, still lit, was lying on its side on his desk.

The man was crying. Old men's tears ran down his cheeks.

'Please. Don't kill me,' he begged. 'I don't know! I'm telling you, I don't know!' he screamed.

The two shots, when they came, sounded no louder than the pops from a child's toy cap gun. The man slumped forward, his face pressing into his once-prized antique Persian rug, his blood mingling with the red dye in its intricate pattern.

'Not so freakin' clever now,' the figure said and kicked out, turning the body over so that the man's face was visible.

'Bastard.' He spat on the lifeless body.

The old man looked strangely at peace.

Chapter 2

Darkness, like a blanket of blackness, was holding her tightly. It was almost squeezing the air out of her lungs. She had lost track of time.

The floor was hard and rough. She was bound hand and foot. The plastic ties were cutting into her skin. She had given up trying to fight them.

The uneven wooden floor under her hands that she had felt, looking for something, anything to help her escape, had suggested she was in some sort of barn. A faint smell of something animal lingered in the air.

She shivered. There was no fresh air, but she was cold and she was trying not to be scared. Trying, but not succeeding. With every passing minute her fear was growing. She had so many questions. Why had they grabbed her? What were they going to do to her? Being left alone had only increased her terror.

Her skimpy T-shirt, tied off above her waist leaving her midriff uncovered, offered her little protection against the low temperature. Her shorts, which had seemed a bit of fun, now only meant her legs were icy cold. She was shivering, uncontrollably. The only sounds were the clicking and chattering of her teeth and the gentle tapping of tiny scurrying feet somewhere nearby. And in the distance, she thought she could hear a soft whooshing sound of wind blowing through trees.

She was aware of the sound of ragged breathing but it was only her own. She was alone. There was occasional whimpering too but that was no animal. It was her. No one else was here. Now. But they would be back. They wouldn't just leave her to starve to death, would they? She didn't know which she feared more – that they would come back or that they wouldn't.

When she had first been brought here and dumped down on the floor, she had shouted and screamed and kicked out wildly. Her feet had connected with the knee of one of her captors. That had only meant a slap across her face which had stung her into silence.

She heard a noise and held her breath. The door scraped open and she felt a light breeze touch her skin, bringing the smell of outside with it. Someone was coming.

'Please, don't,' she said as bright light from a torch hit her full in the eyes, blinding her.

She saw a flash of the tip of a knife inches away from her face.

'Please,' she begged again.

She could make out the dark shape of a man behind it. But only a shape. He had no features, just a black nothingness where his face should be. He didn't speak but she could hear his excited breathing.

A scream rang out through the emptiness, echoing off the walls and fading into the darkness. She hadn't thought she had a scream left in her.

She had felt no pain at first, just the sensation of hot liquid running down over her hand. Her blood. The pain came later.

Chapter 3

'Are you sure it's DCI Gawn Girvin you mean?' the chief constable, Nigel Huntingdon, asked, struggling up into a sitting position in the bed, groggy at having been roused in the middle of his night's sleep. He shook his head, a frown slowly creasing his brow. His wife stirred in the bed beside him but didn't wake, long used to phone calls at all hours of the night.

'I have a lot of excellent officers, sir,' the chief constable said. 'Girvin's been on a career break for a year and she's not even due back on duty for a couple of weeks yet. She may not even be in the country, for all I know. She and her husband have been living in America.'

That's what he'd been told. His caller couldn't see his face. It was just as well. The chief constable didn't like being put on the spot or feeling someone else was making decisions for him. But he knew this call wasn't a request, it was an order.

'I haven't met her, of course, sir, but I've read her file,' he continued, rubbing the sleep out of his eyes. 'I know she's experienced. She's a good detective. Tenacious. Some might say foolhardy even.'

He allowed something that sounded almost like a laugh to escape from his mouth at his admission.

'And she has a commendable clear-up rate, but she can be a bit, shall we say, headstrong?' He hesitated. 'She can go a bit rogue. Or so I've been warned. Once you set her off, you'll not be able to control her.'

His caller had listened, in silence, just breathing evenly. Now he spoke. There was no hesitation or uncertainty in his voice.

'Let me worry about that,' the caller said. 'All you need to know is she is eminently suitable, you might even say, essential, for this investigation. And she is in the country, Chief Constable. She and her husband returned two weeks ago.'

The policeman was wide awake now. He was surprised at this news. This man knew more about his officers than he did.

'I'll get my ACC to contact her and ask her to come in,' he responded.

'Ask! Is that how you run things? Just get her there.'

Without another word, the call was disconnected.

Chapter 4

The faceless man had bandaged her arm and given her something to eat. All without a word being spoken.

He had thrust a floppy paper plate towards her. She took a tentative bite. It was cold and chewy, leathery. She thought it might have started out as lasagne but it could have been anything. She didn't really care what it tasted like. She didn't know how long it had been since she'd had any food. She could vaguely remember a burger at a fast-food restaurant. The thought of its meaty flavour made her salivate.

The man had untied her hands to let her eat but he didn't offer her a fork or knife, nothing she could use as a weapon or to help her escape. Her fingers were tingling with pins and needles from the release of the tight binding as her blood flowed freely into her hands again. After that first bite, she had grabbed handfuls of the food and stuffed it into her mouth. He had watched her as she devoured the tasteless gelatinous mess, the only sound her grunts of satisfaction. She noticed his beady eyes through a slit in his ski mask drilling into her. She could imagine him smiling under the mask. She could imagine his satisfaction to see her like this.

As soon as she had finished the last mouthful, he had grasped her by the arm and dug his nails into her skin, making her squeal. She heard the same scraping sound of the door dragging against the uneven floor. The other man was coming back. What had they planned for her now?

The woman was now lying on the floor, curled up like a baby in its mother's womb. She turned her head to look towards the sound. Light streamed in from behind a figure standing in the doorway. It took a second for her eyes to adjust. She could see empty animal stalls and bales of hay stacked up in the corner beside the door.

A second figure walked slowly towards her. He was tall. Big. Broad-shouldered. His heavy footsteps thudded on the bare wood. She could feel the vibrations through her body. He was dressed all in black with a balaclava covering his head. She had a vague memory of seeing men dressed like this before.

'Get her sitting up!'

She was grabbed by the arm again and pulled roughly up into a sitting position. The man dragged her backwards until he was able to place her like a rag doll propped up against the wall. She did nothing to resist. He handed her a large piece of cardboard.

'Hold that up and smile nicely for the camera, princess,' he ordered.

She knew there must be something written on the card but she couldn't see what it was. She wasn't going to try to turn it around. She didn't want to do anything to annoy them. She blinked as the man took a photograph of her. Then the card was snatched from her hands and a newspaper replaced it.

'Same again, princess,' the man said. 'Smile nicely for your fans.'

Why was he calling her princess? No one had called her that for years. Only one person had ever called her that, and everyone knew he was dead.

Chapter 5

Monday

In an isolated area of Belfast International Airport, far away from the bustle of the busy terminal building, three men stood waiting silently in a cavernous hangar on the edge of the runway. They were watching for the arrival of a private plane. Each was scanning the horizon trying to see through the low cloud which was just beginning to disappear with the early morning sun. A fourth figure stood, slightly apart, talking quietly into his mobile phone and watching his three companions.

'That must be him now, sir,' one of the men said.

He was the youngest of the trio, his striped tie adding a jarring touch of colour to the otherwise grey look of the three suited figures. The speaker was pointing to a small dot high in the sky. Gradually they could identify it as a silver and blue, twin-prop aircraft on approach to the runway. It had appeared in the distance like a tiny beam from a torch peeking through the cloud cover as the rays of the sun reflected off its fuselage. It had no markings. They watched as it grew bigger. The men stood in silence.

Sir Patrick Montgomery, the tallest one of them, held his hand up to shield his eyes from a ray of bright sunlight which had just broken through, portending a sunny day ahead. He wanted to be sure it was the correct plane before making a move. He never acted without having control of a situation. He was a man who left nothing to chance.

Montgomery's mane of thick wavy grey hair was swept back from his face. His matching handlebar moustache and broad sideburns gave him a faintly Victorian look. He would stand out in any crowd. His expression was blank. His dark eyes were hooded, giving nothing away. There were no smile lines around his eyes or mouth. He didn't do much smiling. Instead, his mouth was held firmly shut as if he didn't want to divulge any secrets, almost as if his lips had been sewn together.

Soon the plane would be on the ground.

'They're not expecting any other private planes until later this morning, sir,' the speaker added.

'Well, let's get over there and meet them then,' Montgomery said.

His voice was flat and emotionless but he spoke with a natural authority that assumes unquestioning obedience. He turned on his heel and walked off at a quick pace. His two companions scurried after him. The fourth man, his whispered phone call hastily finished, soon caught them up and hurried along beside them. He was the odd one out of the four. His green uniform brought a touch of brightness to the group. It was the uniform of the deputy chief constable of the Police Service of Northern Ireland.

Chapter 6

Gawn Girvin was in a good mood. Exercise always had that effect on her.

She was just coming towards the end of her morning run. She was breathing a little heavily. Too many rich meals and lots of lying about on the beach reading meant she had spent the last two weeks since they'd got back to Northern Ireland trying to get back to fighting fitness.

She was leaning on the bright blue metal railings at Fisherman's Quay before the final short dash home for a hot shower and some coffee. If she was lucky, Sebastian, her husband, would be waiting with the coffee ready brewed. He might even join her in the shower if he wasn't already engrossed in his latest book. When he got the idea for a new plot, he lost track of time and disappeared into his study for hours.

Her home was hidden from view behind a red-brick Edwardian railway property which had been restored as a private house. Most people wouldn't even know it was there. The modern three-storey villa was perched right on the edge of Belfast Lough. It was spectacular but she still couldn't quite think of it as home.

It took some getting used to. Seb had designed it himself. It was his dream upside-down home. A gym and swim spa in the basement and a study with lots of space for all his books had been his main priorities. The wall of windows in the open-plan room on the top floor, which overlooked the sea and gave a panoramic view stretching from the iconic yellow cranes of Belfast down to the mouth of the lough, was for her.

But so much about her life still felt strange. For the past year, when she had woken in the morning it had been to the sight of a vast empty Pacific Ocean and surfers in colourful boardwalk shorts on the stretch of white sand in front of their rented house, ready to catch some waves. Here her view was a busy seaway with container ships and cruise liners and the regular ferries back and forth to Scotland and England. It was familiar and yet not quite so familiar anymore. And, after the seemingly continuous sunshine of southern California, she wasn't used to the temperature here again – even though it was almost spring – and the greyness when the sun didn't appear. She even found herself missing the greeting of 'Have a nice day' from strangers who you knew didn't really care what kind of day you had. Just hearing the words made you feel a little better about the world, a world which was so warped and twisted and dark. Her world anyway.

The early morning commuter traffic to Belfast was just starting to build up behind her. She felt, rather than heard, the whoosh as cars sped by on the Marine Highway using every bit of the permitted forty miles per hour and more.

She had stopped at the Airstream coffee truck in its usual spot in the town's main car park under the shadow of the Norman castle's battlements. It looked incongruously modern and shiny against the medieval backdrop. She had bought herself a double espresso, a needed boost for the final push, and chatted to the woman behind the counter. She had patted the friendly dog belonging to an elderly man waiting in the short queue which had formed even though it was early. Gawn could almost convince herself it was possible for her to have a normal life here again. Whatever normal meant for her.

As she finished the last drops of coffee and tossed the paper cup into a handy litter bin, she felt her smart watch vibrate. She had run a little further and been away a little longer than usual. Seb would be waiting for her, worried that something had happened.

In the first weeks in California, he had been on edge, watching constantly for signs that Gawn's recent brush with a maniac was not continuing to affect her. Gradually she had relaxed and so had he. But she hadn't forgotten any of it. Every second of the time spent at the monster's mercy was etched in her memory. She would never forget it. But since they had been back in Northern Ireland, Seb had been over-attentive again.

'Yes, darling?' she said into the watch, without looking down.

'Gawn. It's me. Anne Wilkinson.'

The woman hadn't needed to add her name. Gawn had recognised her voice right away. ACC Anne Wilkinson was her boss, the head of the Crime Department in the PSNI. They hadn't spoken for a year, but she knew that unique mixture of Geordie accent, now tinged with an unmistakeable Belfast intonation.

She was embarrassed at addressing her boss as 'darling' but she was even more puzzled about why Wilkinson was phoning her.

'Ma'am?'

Saying the word sounded strange. She hadn't called anyone ma'am for a year and had flinched for the first few weeks in LA when restaurant servers and shopkeepers had greeted her that way. Yet the response had come automatically to her this morning.

'I know you're not due back on duty for another couple of weeks but I need you on a new case.' The woman sounded genuinely apologetic.

A lifetime of service, first in the army and then the police, meant there was only one response Gawn could make. Her words were almost automatic, a reaction rather than a decision. She didn't take time to consider. It didn't matter why or how Wilkinson needed help or even what Gawn knew Seb's reaction would be to the news, she responded the only way she knew how.

Chapter 7

The woman pulled herself up into a sitting position on the hard floor. She sat cross-legged, like a child. She was trying to remember all that had happened to her. Her arm was aching, making it hard to think. Blood had seeped through the crude bandage. Her head was throbbing and she was thirsty.

Bits and pieces started to come back to her. She could remember two men appearing at their door. They had seemed like friendly locals. That's what she had thought. Then suddenly she had been grabbed from behind. She remembered the hands holding her arms pinioned behind her, feeling as if they were going to be pulled from their sockets. Something had been put over her face. She remembered the feel of the rough cloth and a pin prick in her arm. In her last moments of consciousness, she saw Norrie talking to one of the men. Then there was nothing more until she had woken up in the darkness here, alone.

Where was Norrie? The woman allowed herself to cry. She couldn't be strong. She was frightened. She couldn't be brave without Norrie. Tears flowed down her face. She sobbed. But there was no one to hear her.

Chapter 8

'What does that bloody woman want? Why does she need your help? You're not the only chief inspector in the PSNI, are you? They've managed without you for a year. You were supposed to be having a phased return to work, to be eased back into the job behind a desk over a few weeks. Now she calls and you just come running.'

Sebastian was pacing up and down along the wall of glass overlooking the channel. Gawn noticed a container ship making its way slowly down the lough just over his shoulder. He was like a caged animal. Fear was making him angry. His normally sunny face was marred in an all-encompassing, ugly frown.

Gawn had known he would be furious. She knew he had secretly hoped that such a long break from her job would convince her to give it up altogether. They didn't need the money. His contract with the movie studio had been renewed for at least two more seasons and his books were selling well. If she had fallen pregnant while they'd been away, she knew she would have stayed and concentrated on being a good mother rather than chasing bad guys. But that hadn't happened for them.

She was back in Northern Ireland and she was going back to work. It wasn't quite the way she had anticipated it, but maybe it was better that she didn't have days to worry about her first day back: what it would be like, how people might treat her. She knew some of her colleagues would be wary of her. She had never been a popular figure: too demanding, and not 'one of the boys'.

'I don't know what this is about yet, Seb. I only know it must be serious otherwise she wouldn't have phoned like this. Someone's in trouble and someone from one of my old cases is involved in some way. That's why she wants me to head up the investigation. But that's all she told me.'

Gawn had watched her husband's handsome face as she had tried to explain. She knew it wasn't much of an explanation. Wilkinson had told her very little. She had mentioned a problem with senior staffing levels and staff illness, and something about Gawn's experience making her suitable, but she hadn't gone into any detail. Instead, she had asked Gawn to meet with her urgently in her office. This morning. As soon as possible.

Not wanting to argue with him, Gawn turned away towards the stairs down to the bedrooms. She would grab a quick shower and change into something more suitable than the tracksuit she was currently wearing. She couldn't show up at Police HQ dressed like this.

'You're going right now?' Seb asked. He sounded incredulous. 'Just like that? Wilkinson clicks her fingers and that's it. You come running.'

'She wants me right away.'

'Right. *She* wants. And what about what I want, Gawn? Am I allowed any say in this at all?' His voice was loud. He was almost shouting at her, something he never did.

Gawn turned back to face him. She had been going to tell him her work was none of his business but, when she saw the fear written across his face, she knew everything she did was his business. Of course, it was. Everything she did affected him too. He wasn't trying to control her. He wasn't angry with her. He loved her and he was worried about her. Did she want him not to care?

She hurried back across the room and put her arms around his waist, snuggling into him. After a second's hesitation, he hugged her back, holding her close as if he would never let her go.

'I'll be alright, you know. It's my work. It's me. It's always been me, Seb. It was nice to get that break away from everything and recharge my batteries but that wasn't real life. It was just a sort of extended dream holiday. I think we both knew all along I'd go back to work, didn't we? You knew what a badass cop you were taking on when you married me, Sebastian York. I can't change. I'll never change.'

Her words had brought a smile to his face. 'Badass cop' was one of his nicknames for her. She reached up and allowed her lips to brush against his. His mouth began to respond passionately but she pushed back from him and he let her go.

She smiled and raised her left eyebrow to him, in a way well-known to her colleagues when she was waiting for a response to some tricky question she had posed. He smiled weakly back at her and sighed. He was still worried, but she knew she had won the argument. He wouldn't try to stop her.

Chapter 9

Gawn was formally dressed in a smart navy trouser suit and plain white silk shirt which had been hanging in her wardrobe for a year. When she had looked in the mirror, she was like the tall, confident red head with a reputation for toughness she had been back then.

She might look confident but that wasn't how she felt.

As she drove up the busy Newtownards Road to Police HQ she allowed herself an occasional glance around. It was all so familiar and yet so strange, almost like scenes from some old movie she had watched.

All too soon, she had navigated the busy junction at Knock Road and, before she had fully prepared herself mentally, Gawn was making the turn into Brooklyn House, police headquarters. The high brick wall sheltered the complex from the sight of curious passing drivers and the threat of terrorist attacks. The fluttering PSNI flag at full mast, the huge name sign, and the PSNI insignia mounted to the side of the opening, brought a smile of familiarity to her face. Her stomach tightened as she saw the administrative building in front of her and knew the moment had come.

Gawn had no police ID on her so she had to stop at the barrier and explain who she was and why she was there. The armed PC on duty didn't recognise her. He checked his list of expected visitors, put a tick against her name, searched the boot of her car and then waved her through to the visitors car park.

Inside, Gawn walked along the corridor to Wilkinson's office, her steps echoing on the tiled flooring in time to the heavier clump of the boots of the young PC who was escorting her through the building. That felt strange. She glanced down at the visitor's name badge on her lapel. She was not just some casual visitor.

'Come in.'

The familiar figure of Anne Wilkinson, dwarfed behind a huge desk, a leftover from her predecessor's days, was the first thing she saw. The woman looked well, if a little older than the last time they had met. There were a few more touches of grey in her short dark hair, a few more worry lines around her eyes. But those eyes were smiling. Maybe it wasn't so serious.

Wilkinson greeted her warmly, walking around the desk to shake hands. 'You're looking very fit and well, Gawn. The tan certainly suits you.'

Gawn was surprised. She hadn't expected any small talk.

'Thank you, ma'am,' Gawn said.

Wilkinson walked over to the window and stood looking out, her back towards the room and her hands clenched tightly behind her.

'I'm just watching out for a visitor. When he arrives, we'll be needed in the conference room.' She seemed to be about to say more when she saw something in the car park below which caught her attention. 'Ah, this must be our VIP now. Right. Let's go, Chief Inspector.'

Gawn almost flinched to hear herself addressed as 'chief inspector' in these surroundings.

Just as they were about to leave the room, with her hand resting on the door handle, Wilkinson turned to face her.

'I do appreciate you coming in today, Gawn. I know you weren't due back on duty yet. And then it was meant to be desk duties and a phased return to work.' The ACC sighed loudly. 'I'm afraid I can't offer you any of that. You'll be thrown straight into the thick of it.'

There was an expression on the woman's face Gawn couldn't quite interpret but it made her wonder what 'it' was.

Gawn couldn't help feeling even more nervous now. What the hell was going on?

Chapter 10

There had been no chat between the two women as they walked along. The ACC, shoulders back, head held high, strode ahead looking straight in front of her, almost as if she was in a passing-out parade. Gawn towered over her in her usual high heels. Wilkinson was in her regulation flat shoes, highly polished of course. Gawn had never found those shoes flattering.

Wilkinson knocked at the heavy oak door then walked straight in without waiting for a response. It seemed that everyone had been waiting just for them; waiting for her, Gawn thought. She felt annoyed that she seemed to be the only one who didn't know what was going on.

The room was full of bodies, big men, filling the space with wafts of spicy aftershave vying with testosterone. Four sombre-looking men in PSNI uniforms were already seated at the highly polished table in the centre of the room facing them when they walked in. They had looked up at the newcomers but their serious expressions hadn't changed.

Gawn recognised the chief constable. He was new. She'd never met him, but she'd seen him on television responding to whatever new crisis the police service was facing. He was flanked by Chief Superintendent Ronnie Clarke of Special Operations and Superintendent Harry Floyd from the Intelligence Branch. She had come across them both before, thankfully from a distance. The other man sitting at the table with them was wearing the uniform of the deputy chief constable. Gawn didn't recognise him. He must be new too.

No introductions were made. The men's faces were inscrutable, like masks, giving nothing away. A trickle of perspiration made its way down the back of Gawn's neck, even though it wasn't particularly hot in the room.

Another row of men in business suits was sitting facing the police officers. They had their backs to the door but one had craned round to inspect the newcomers when they walked in. His eyes had met Gawn's and he had almost smiled at her.

Two uniformed armed officers stood at the end of the room trying, and failing, to be inconspicuous. Their Heckler & Koch MP5 machine guns were held at an angle across their bodies. They looked relaxed but Gawn knew they would be ready to spring into action if needed. She had never seen such an overtly armed guard inside an office at a meeting in Police HQ before. She hadn't even brought her personal protection pistol with her. What was going on? Was there some imminent terrorist attack? Had she been mentioned in some threat? Was Seb in danger? Her mind was going into overdrive.

'Have a seat,' the chief constable said without preamble and gestured to two empty chairs at the end of the table directly in front of the armed guards. It sounded less of an invitation and more of an order even though it had been delivered in a soft Norfolk burr. He waited until they had sat down, and Wilkinson had removed her hat and set it on the table in front of her before he spoke again. His voice was deep and sonorous, filling the room.

'This is Assistant Chief Constable Anne Wilkinson, Mr Ambassador.'

The chief constable was looking directly at the man sitting opposite him, in the middle of the row of civilians.

'She heads our Crime Department, as I've explained to you, and this is Detective Chief Inspector Gawn Girvin, from the Serious Crime unit, one of our best detectives.' He gave an almost imperceptible nod of his head in Gawn's direction. 'ACC Wilkinson and I have already discussed your situation and we feel DCI Girvin and her team would be best placed to take charge of dealing with it.'

The chief constable had been directing all his comments to the distinguished-looking middle-aged man sitting directly across from him but Gawn had noticed his momentary glance at the big man sitting beside the ambassador.

Gawn had listened with a mounting sense of astonishment at what she was hearing. The VIP was an ambassador. Perhaps that was why she had been chosen. Gawn had worked in the Metropolitan Police's Parliamentary and Diplomatic Protection Unit for a time. She had never heard any senior officer describe her as 'one of our best detectives' before and, with a suspicion born of long years of senior officers passing the buck, she wondered what she was being lined up for. What exactly was this man's 'situation'?

Chapter 11

The distinguished-looking little man in the middle of the group of suits was introduced as Ambassador Jorgen Pedersen from Norway. His mouth formed the merest suggestion of a smile and he nodded his head graciously in acknowledgement of the women.

Pedersen was a long-faced man with a pasty complexion. His greying hair was thinning and he had resorted to a comb-over style to conceal a bald patch. His eyes had a rheumy look and his brow was furrowed as if he was in pain. His hands were clenched together on the table, and although he was trying to appear casual, the whiteness of his knuckles showed how tense he was.

The large, grey-haired hulk of a man sitting beside the ambassador, spoke next. He had not yet been introduced. Gawn had noticed him as soon as she had come into the room. He was hard to miss. Not only was he big and broad-shouldered but she had been almost mesmerised by his bushy moustache and his matching sideburns. They were distinctive. He was distinctive. She had noticed that fleeting interaction with the chief constable and wondered what it meant.

The man introduced himself as Sir Patrick Montgomery from the Department for Business and Trade. His accent was English public school. He carried with him that innate confidence and assurance of superiority Gawn had come across before in the senior ranks of both the Met and the army.

'Ambassador Pedersen and I are old friends from my time spent in our embassy in Oslo,' Montgomery explained. He turned to look at the ambassador with an encouraging expression on his face, or what Gawn thought must pass for one from him. He patted Pedersen on the shoulder as if to signal it was his turn to speak.

The ambassador took a pristine white handkerchief out of his top pocket and dabbed his forehead. He began speaking in a low, hesitant voice.

'Chief Inspector, are you aware of the Nina and Norrie travel channel on YouTube?'

Gawn was taken completely off guard. This wasn't what she'd been expecting to be asked. She wasn't sure exactly what she had been expecting, but not this.

Pedersen waited for just a second before continuing, obviously assuming a positive response. 'Everyone these days seems to be a fan. Except me,' he added with a self-deprecating smile which he shared with the four PSNI officers opposite him.

His English was almost perfect with hardly a trace of an accent but she thought he was trying too hard to seem relaxed. The jibe at himself had been contrived. She could imagine he'd used it before.

'Not really, sir, I'm afraid. It's not my thing,' Gawn admitted.

'Then you won't have heard of Nina and Norrie,' he said.

She hadn't, and her face provided an answer without her having to say anything.

'They're an internet sensation.' He made the phrase sound like a criticism. 'Apparently,' the ambassador added and sighed loudly.

Gawn had no idea where this was going. Who were these people he was talking about? It was as if he had heard her unspoken question as he said, without prompting, 'Norrie is my son, Chief Inspector.'

Pedersen was looking directly at her and she could see he was very worried.

'He's missing,' he said eventually. 'They both are.'

Chapter 12

'They haven't uploaded anything for several days,' Pedersen continued.

'Is that unusual, sir?' Gawn asked.

'Oh, yes. Normally they put some new piece of nonsense online every day or every couple of days at least. It's how they make their living. Norrie dropped out of university against his mother's and my wishes after he met Nina. He was doing his PhD,' he explained.

The ambassador seemed to have difficulty saying the woman's name without it sounding like a curse on his tongue.

'We cut off his allowance,' Pedersen said. 'We thought that would bring him to his senses. If he had no money, and we knew his girlfriend had none, then he would come running home. But, instead, they got this crazy idea of travelling around filming themselves and sharing every little detail of their lives with their so-called followers.'

'Subscribers and patrons, sir,' one of his staff said, interrupting the ambassador.

Pedersen shrugged. 'Whatever they're called. They bought an old campervan and painted it up. Nina fancies herself as an artist of sorts. A street artist, I suppose you would call it. They've been living off what they get from their followers and sponsors and they're supposed to be writing a book about their travels.'

'And now you think something must have happened to them because they've stopped posting online?' Gawn asked.

'Yes. They wouldn't just stop,' Pedersen assured her. 'They couldn't afford to. How would they live?'

'Have you tried to contact them, sir?' Gawn asked. It seemed an obvious question but she had to ask it.

'Of course. But they aren't taking our calls. Both my wife and I have tried. We had a big row with Norrie last month and I think he must have changed his number after that. It's just ringing out when we try to phone.'

Gawn was beginning to wonder whether this was really a case for Serious Crime. A missing person didn't usually merit this kind of attention, at least at first. A fit and healthy young couple, with no obvious reason to be regarded as vulnerable, wouldn't. There had to be more to it.

These were two adults who had chosen to live a rather bohemian lifestyle somewhat off-grid. There had been a serious falling-out with the boy's parents and they were now blanking them. That sort of thing happened in families all the time. It didn't seem to merit this amount of attention from such senior people and she was sure it wouldn't have received it if Mr Pedersen had been just that, *Mister* Pedersen, instead of Ambassador Pedersen. Nina and Norrie had probably gone off somewhere; had enough of their precarious lifestyle and moved on to make a living some other way but the PSNI wouldn't want to risk something happening to them on their patch.

'What about Nina's parents?' Gawn asked. 'Have you tried contacting them?'

'Her parents are dead,' Pedersen said. 'She's an only child. As far as we know, anyway. I think that was part of the attraction for my son. He's always seen himself as some sort of romantic hero rescuing damsels. Don Quixote in the twenty-first century.' Pedersen's voice sounded scathing.

'We've already checked the ferries and the hospitals in case they've had an accident or maybe left the country out of Belfast or Larne but there was nothing. No trace of them,' Montgomery interjected.

Gawn was surprised. What had Montgomery to do with this? Why was he checking hospitals and ferries?

'The Irish police have been most cooperative. The two arrived in Ireland just about a month ago and spent a little time in the Republic. They came north over the border ten days ago. They uploaded a video from Fermanagh Lakelands and others from Derry and a day they spent at the North Coast at Dunluce Castle. The last one was from the Antrim Coast Road on their way to Carrickfergus. They promised to post from the castle there and then, nothing. They just stopped,' Montgomery said, and he just stopped too.

Gawn realised, while Montgomery was talking, that he was heavily involved and he had obvious influence. It seemed he had been in touch with An Garda Síochána and had had people, either his own or maybe the PSNI, checking with hospitals and ports. Who was he exactly? Department for Business and Trade? Somehow, she was beginning to doubt that.

'Is it possible they just went back over the border and are somewhere there now and maybe they've got themselves jobs or something?' Gawn asked.

Pedersen pulled a face.

Superintendent Floyd answered, even though her question had not been directed to him. 'I suppose that might have been a possibility, Chief Inspector, but we have reason to think it's not the case.'

Gawn knew his people were used to carrying out covert surveillance and intelligence gathering. She realised it would probably have been his team who had provided Montgomery with the details of when the couple had crossed the border into Northern Ireland and that they hadn't crossed back.

'They live in a campervan, as you've heard,' Floyd said. 'They painted it up with fairies and cartoon characters. It's not exactly unobtrusive, Chief Inspector. You could spot it a mile away. We picked it up easily on camera when they were coming into Fermanagh so I think they would have been easy enough to spot crossing back over if they'd headed down south again.'

Unless they were trying not to be seen, Gawn thought to herself. Possible explanations for their disappearance ran through her mind. Perhaps they had sold or ditched the van or even repainted it in a plain colour. Perhaps they'd crashed it and sold what was left of it to some car dismantler. They could have travelled by bus or car instead. Or even flown out. But she thought Montgomery would have had all that checked. Underestimating this man would be a mistake.

Gawn hadn't led too many missing persons investigations and this one would be high profile – two foreigners and one of them the son of an ambassador. As she was considering her priorities for action, there was something in Pedersen's face that made her pause. He had more to say, and she didn't like the way this was going.

'Is there something else you'd like to tell me, sir?'

What she really wanted to say was, 'What the hell is going on? What has happened that you aren't telling me?' but she didn't.

She locked eyes with Pedersen instead.

Pedersen took two pages from a folder sitting in front of him on the table and glanced down at them before sliding them along towards Gawn and Wilkinson.

One glance was all it took. Gawn heard Wilkinson draw in her breath sharply. The page was A4 – white, ordinary printer paper. Nothing distinctive. It was a photocopy of two pictures of a girl, presumably Nina. She was sitting on a bare floor. She was looking straight at the camera. Her hair was dishevelled and the tracks of recent tears were plain to see on her face. There was a mark on her cheek which looked like she had been hit, and a bandage around her lower arm stained with what looked like blood.

Between the two photographs there were seven words printed in heavy black marker.

We have them. We'll be in touch.

Chapter 13

This wasn't a missing persons case. It was a kidnapping, and a high profile one. They should expect a ransom demand.

Gawn was seething. They had been playing games with her. They had wasted time before telling her what was going on and, even now, she suspected she might be getting only part of the story. But at least she felt on slightly firmer ground. Criminals she knew. Criminals she could deal with. Criminals she could track down and catch.

'When did you receive this, Mr Ambassador?' Gawn asked holding the page out, trying not to sound too accusatory.

She realised what she had was only a photocopy. The original would be off somewhere, being tested. She had noticed two black streaks at the side of the page. Perhaps the lab could find something to help them identify an area to start a search.

Pedersen grimaced. 'It was left under the windscreen wipers on my car last night.'

'Your official car? In London?' Gawn asked.

'No. My personal car. My wife and I were visiting friends for dinner. I had driven us there myself.'

'What about your bodyguard?'

'He was inside the house with us. He was in the kitchen while we were eating. He didn't see anything.'

'Your friends must have a home security system.'

'Of course they do. I watched the footage and passed it to Sir Patrick last night.'

'It shows a figure on a bicycle stopping for just a second beside the ambassador's car and slipping that message under the wipers,' Montgomery told her. 'Then he pedals off across the road and onto Hampstead Heath. We have a copy of the footage for you.'

A USB drive was passed along the table to her. She was sure experts of all kinds were vetting the video even while they were sitting here discussing it.

'No fingerprints on the wipers or anywhere on the car?' she asked.

'No. He rested his hand on the bonnet of the car to steady himself as he was putting the message under the wipers, but he was wearing gloves. You'll see that in the footage,' Montgomery said.

'Why are you so sure this has a Belfast connection, sir?' Gawn asked. 'That they're still here somewhere? They could be in London, being held somewhere there.'

It was Montgomery who broke in again to answer her question.

'Ambassador Pedersen contacted me as soon as he found the note.'

Montgomery didn't explain why the ambassador had done that. Gawn found the action surprising. She would have expected him to contact the police. That would surely have been a more normal reaction. But little seemed normal about what was going on.

'I contacted the Met commissioner immediately and he had the original message sent to the lab and the photographs blown up to give as much background detail as possible. As soon as I saw them, I sent them on to your chief constable. Look at it yourself, Chief Inspector.'

Another sheet of paper was passed along to her. Wilkinson looked over Gawn's shoulder at the page. They could see a tiny part of the original photograph. It was blurry, from the magnification, but it was of a small section of the doorway to the side of the girl's head. Gawn recognised the view – the two towering yellow cranes were synonymous with the city. It had been taken somewhere near Belfast.

Gawn was looking at Montgomery with new eyes. At first, she had thought him just another pompous civil servant. He had said he was Pedersen's friend. But she believed there was more to their relationship and, from what he had said and how he had reacted to the ambassador's message, for all his talk of the Department for Business, she now suspected he was from the Security Services.

'There's no reason to suspect any terrorist connection to the abduction, Chief Inspector,' Montgomery said and looked across the table.

'What do you suspect then, Sir Patrick?' Gawn asked.

She thought she might as well direct her questions to him. He was the puppet master in this scene, she had realised. Not Pedersen and not even the chief constable.

Gawn had posed the question to Montgomery but she was surprised when it was the ambassador who replied. He placed his hand on Montgomery's arm to stop him from speaking.

'It is possible—' the man hesitated, then continued '—that Nina is involved in this. My wife and I never trusted her. She was always secretive. We don't even know her last name. We always suspected she had a background with drugs.

'It is also possible—' Pedersen paused again for a longer time before going on '—it is also possible that Norrie could be involved too. He is very much under her influence, Chief Inspector. Ever since they met, he's changed. He's a different boy and it's possible she's convinced him that they can get money out of us by hiding out and pretending to be kidnapped.'

Gawn could see how difficult it was for him to admit this about his son. She knew how keen he and the British government would be to bring this to a speedy conclusion without involving the press if it was all just a scam cooked up by the young couple themselves to extort money from his family. So far, all they had was a picture of Nina. She was still alive. Or at least she had been when the photo was taken yesterday, according to the date on the newspaper she had been clutching. But there was no sign of Norrie. Why not? Could the ambassador's suspicions be correct? Could he be behind this?

'Either way, sir, real or scam, we should be expecting a ransom demand. Sooner rather than later. I presume the Met has a trace on Mr Pedersen's phone.'

Montgomery nodded. 'Superintendent Lynch. Matthew Lynch – I think you know him – is in charge at the London end.'

He had done his homework. He knew about her, about her career, about her time in London. Was Montgomery the reason she had been called in?

Yes, she knew Lynch.

'I'll get started trying to find where they are and who's holding them. If anyone is,' she said.

Sometimes parents had a good idea of what was going on in their children's lives and sometimes they hadn't a clue. She thought with Pedersen it might be the latter.

Chapter 14

'What do you think, Gawn?' Wilkinson asked. She fixed Gawn with an openly curious stare.

They were back in her office, seated either side of her desk. Gawn suspected more talking would be going on in the conference room, now they were out of the way.

'I think I'm bloody angry, ma'am.'

At Gawn's words and tone, Wilkinson's head jerked up and her eyes widened in surprise.

'Not with you, ma'am,' Gawn added hastily. 'They spent time pussyfooting around in there, didn't they? Instead of "my son and his girlfriend have been kidnapped and here's a photo which makes us think it happened here", we got that whole run around first. And the Met and Lynch are going to be poking into everything too.'

'You know this Superintendent Lynch, do you?' Wilkinson asked.

'Yes.'

'Well?'

'Well enough. He was my boss in the Diplomatic Unit for a while when I was there. He was a chief inspector then.'

'Will you be able to work with him?'

'I don't have very much choice, do I, ma'am? He has the only piece of original evidence in the case. The ransom note. But I imagine Montgomery will make sure he cooperates. Unless that doesn't suit his agenda, of course.'

'You think Montgomery has an agenda?' Wilkinson asked, her head cocked slightly to one side like a nervous little bird.

Gawn wasn't fooled. She knew Wilkinson was a canny copper. She was experienced and knew all about the politics of senior rank. She would have her own suspicions even if she hadn't been included in all the discussions between Montgomery and the chief constable.

'Don't you?' Gawn said. 'What's he really doing here? How is he involved? He and the ambassador might be old friends, like he says, but he seems to be taking a very hands-on interest in it all, doesn't he?'

'Look, ma'am, I think Ambassador Pedersen is genuinely worried about his son and scared that he might be part of some scam. I believe that. He probably doesn't know which is worse at the minute – that his son might have been kidnapped or that he might be involved in some sort of shake-down of his own parents.'

'I agree,' Wilkinson said. She sat back in her chair, taking a sip of the coffee she had produced for herself and Gawn. The chief inspector's love of strong coffee was almost legendary.

'You noticed the marks on the photocopy?' Gawn asked.

'Of course. They're probably blood. No doubt for proof of life. But we don't have the original page. Pedersen didn't bring it or rather Montgomery didn't. I'm told the Met's having it tested. If it's blood, I'm sure they'll let us know,' Wilkinson said, trying to sound encouraging.

'Let us know!' Gawn almost exploded, her voice louder than she'd intended. 'Are we running this investigation or are Montgomery and the Met? We should have the original ransom note. Now, ma'am. Potentially important evidence is being held back from us.'

Wilkinson's tone was soothing. 'I know. I know. It's not ideal but you'll have to work with it for now. We can't push back too hard. Not yet. We need Pedersen's cooperation and Montgomery's too. And you need to contact Lynch and get him onside.'

'There's more to all this, isn't there, ma'am?' Gawn asked.

'I think so,' Wilkinson said. 'I do know the chief constable asked for you by name. He phoned me at home early this morning. *Very* early,' she added and shrugged. 'Perhaps it's because of your previous experience with the Met. That's what he intimated to me when he phoned. Or perhaps it's Montgomery who brought you to his attention and I honestly don't know what that means, Gawn.'

Gawn had never met this chief constable. She knew nothing about him. Why would he have asked for her specifically? She didn't believe it was because of her experience with the Diplomatic Unit. Any DCI could liaise with the Met. It didn't need to be her. Her time spent there was as likely to be a disadvantage as an advantage, given her record. She had made enemies. Fortunately, Lynch wasn't one of them. At least she didn't think so.

'He knew you were still on leave but he phoned me anyway and asked me to convince you to come back early. Well, ordered really. I would have given the investigation to someone else even though I don't have any other officer with your experience available or your contacts at the Met. I think you might find both of those rather useful. And you know how spooks work too, I believe.'

Wilkinson didn't say anything else but she gave Gawn a meaningful look. Somewhere in her personnel record, Gawn knew, would be some, mostly redacted, details of her work in Afghanistan. British and American operatives had been there and she had worked with some of them.

'You think the Security Service is involved?' Gawn asked. 'Montgomery?'

'I don't know. Maybe.'

Wilkinson took another sip of coffee. 'We've made some changes while you've been away. All the Serious Crime teams are working out of Castlereagh now so there can be more cross-cooperation and better deployment of personnel. We're short staffed, as I told you. That wasn't just an excuse, I'm afraid.

'There's an office for you there. Paul Maxwell has been keeping your seat warm. He's done a good job but I don't think he'd be quite up to dealing with all the issues this case might throw up. He's too straight.

'He's expecting you. And there's been a few changes in your team too. He'll bring you up to speed.'

Chapter 15

There was a tiny sliver of light sneaking its way in under the door. It must be daytime. Was it the second or third day she had been here? She didn't know. She'd lost count.

She was hungry again and she needed the toilet. The faceless man had freed her hands and feet several times since she had been here and given her a bucket in the corner to use. He had watched her while she used it. She had seen his beady eyes light up through the slit in his balaclava as she had pulled down her shorts and perched over the bucket.

She had tried calling out but after a couple of weak shouts she had given up. No one had appeared. If someone didn't come soon, she would have to soil herself. She didn't want to give them that satisfaction.

What did these bastards want? She didn't have any money. Maybe they expected Norrie to have money or that his parents would pay for their release. Maybe they wouldn't hurt her. They'd need to keep her in good condition to make sure the ransom was paid, wouldn't they?

But where was Norrie? Why were they keeping them apart? It wouldn't have been so bad if she wasn't here by herself; if he was here with her. At least they could have talked. Norrie was always able to make her laugh. He would have had her laughing even here.

Chapter 16

'Welcome back, boss.'

DI Paul Maxwell met Gawn in the corridor outside a door with 'Incident Room A' written on it.

'Paul. Great to see you.'

There was an awkward moment when neither of them seemed to know what to do next. Shaking hands seemed much too formal after all they had been through together, but hugging was not her style and he knew that. So, he gave a small wave of his hand in her direction without moving any closer to her and she smiled warmly back at him.

'I suppose you want to see your office and meet the team. We have some new people you don't know.'

'Yes. But first…'

Before she got the words out, Maxwell finished the sentence for her.

'A cup of coffee,' he said. 'Never fear, boss. We moved all your gear. The coffee's been brewing for you. The cafetière should be just about ready to pour. I'll go and grab a cup of tea and join you.'

She had been going to say that first she would have to phone the Met, but she didn't. She didn't want to disappoint him. He was trying to make her feel welcome.

He was probably trying to hide his disappointment at her return. He would have enjoyed being in charge. It was only natural.

She agreed and watched him walk into the incident room, a blast of chatter sounding through the opened door for the seconds it took until the door closed again. The phone call to the Met could wait. A short while. Not too long.

Her name was on another door just a little way down the corridor. With the next step, over this threshold, she would be back in the situation she had left a year ago. It was in her office – not this one but one almost the same – where she had told Maxwell she was taking a break. She hadn't seen nor spoken to him since. He had not tried to contact her.

The new office was almost a carbon copy of her old one. It looked as if they must have used most of her old furniture. The view from her window was over Ladas Drive across to a busy service station and a low-rise office building. She could see the top of the tall flats at Bell's Bridge roundabout pointing up into a grey sky and knew the house where George Best had grown up was somewhere nearby. It was a tourist attraction and an Airbnb now. Of a Friday evening, she would be able to hear the 'Ravenhill Roar' from the local rugby ground if she opened the window.

Gawn poured herself a cup of coffee and settled into her old revolving chair. It was like putting on a well-worn glove. Maxwell knocked and walked in with a mug in his hand. She noticed it was emblazoned with one word: 'Dad'. She supposed his children must have bought it for him for Father's Day or maybe his birthday. Seb would never have one of those.

'So, how was sunny California?' he asked, smiling. He sat down across from her and took a sip of his tea, then blew across the top of the mug to cool the liquid down.

'Sunny,' she laughed. 'And not home.'

'You're glad to be back, then, boss?'

Maxwell didn't just mean to Northern Ireland.

'Yes. I'm afraid I might be a bit rusty for a day or two, but we have a case already so bring me up to speed on the team. Who's gone and who's new?'

Chapter 17

Gawn stood and looked around the incident room, allowing her gaze to rest momentarily longer on some of the new faces. Maxwell had provided her with mini bios of the new officers. He had assured her they were good. That was enough for her.

The room was a little bigger than the one at their old base, although that could just be her memory playing tricks on her, and it had obviously been recently redecorated, the smell of new paint still lingering in the air.

Everyone looked busy. She was pleased to see DC Jamie Grant looking a little older and, she hoped, a little wiser. DC John – known to everyone as 'Jack' – Dee was there too.

But there was no Walter Pepper, the investigator she had cajoled out of retirement to work with her, and no DC Jo Hill. She had heard Hill was working as a partner in a firm of private investigators in Belfast. DS Erin McKeown was missing too. Maxwell had already explained that she was on secondment to the RCMP.

Then there were the new members of the squad. The lightly tanned thirty-something with long blond hair neatly held back in a bun looked busy, inputting something into her computer, her fingers flying confidently over the keyboard. She must be DS Sian Nolan. Gawn noticed the woman's tight black leather trousers and thought of

Maxwell's comment to her that she wasn't the only diva in their midst now. Gawn had feigned outrage at his words but knew she had been a bit of a handful when she had first arrived and her appearance had drawn comments too.

Across from the sergeant was another new female officer. She couldn't have been more different to Nolan. Where the DS was likely to turn heads wherever she went, this woman was slightly built, almost waif-like. She looked as if she could meld into the furniture and might prefer to do just that. Her mousy coloured hair was pulled back austerely, revealing a pale face and huge brown eyes. This, she realised, was DC Sandra Watt.

Just one more newcomer to meet now. But there was no one else she didn't recognise in the room. DC Rohan Sharma was nowhere in sight. Just when Gawn was going to introduce herself to the team, the door opened behind her and an excited voice shouted, 'She's in the building.' Gawn swung round and saw the shocked face of a young man who had just pushed his way backwards through the doorway into the room, clutching a mug in one hand and balancing a pile of folders in the other. He had taken one look at her and dropped the mug at her feet splashing its contents over his red chinos and smashing the mug. He managed to retain his hold on the folders but he did a sort of little dance as the hot liquid permeated the material of his trousers and burned his legs. His eyebrows disappeared under a shaggy fringe and his mouth formed a shocked O in reaction to the mixture of surprise and pain, but no sound came out.

There was silence in the room. Everyone was looking at Gawn waiting for her reaction. Time seemed to stand still. Then Gawn broke into a laugh and everyone else joined in.

'Quite the entrance. DC Sharma, I presume,' she said.

'I am so, so sorry, ma'am. Did I get any tea over you?' Sharma asked solicitously and moved to kneel down in front of her and wipe her trouser legs. She moved back out of his reach.

'No. I'm fine. But I certainly won't forget our first meeting.'

Sharma smiled uncertainly up at her from his kneeling position and his row of perfectly straight white teeth against his dark skin lit up his face. There was an endearing boyish quality to his features. Maxwell had told her that Sharma was someone who loved figures and statistics, who could be trusted to plod through mounds of information that others would find boring. He was a trained video analyst and he had already proved his value to the team. Gawn thought his skills might be very useful for this case.

Chapter 18

'You all know what to do. I want progress. Quickly. These two have been missing since the weekend. We'll get back together at four. Make sure you have something to report,' Maxwell said, finishing off sternly.

He and Gawn had already decided that, at least for now, he would take the lead. She was still feeling disconcerted at the speed of her return. Less than four hours ago she had been on leave, at home, with nothing more serious on her agenda for the day ahead than whether she should finish the latest book she was reading or watch a documentary about penguins.

She had watched the faces of her team as Maxwell explained they were hunting kidnappers who had seized a Norwegian couple. He hadn't mentioned the Norwegian ambassador nor anything about the involvement of the Metropolitan Police, although she had shared that with him. One or two seemed familiar with internet influencers and Sharma had admitted he'd watched Nina and Norrie when they'd posted about a trip to Wales.

Maxwell had tasked Grant and Sharma to watch their channel while others started work on victimology, delving into the couple's backgrounds. Watt was to begin trawling through their followers and noting any suspicious or threatening comments.

The inspector would contact the local station in Carrickfergus to give them a heads-up. They would need boots on the street asking questions when they had an idea of where the two had been abducted. It seemed that the last place they had been headed to was a fast-food drive-thru. If that was confirmed, they would need to try to track them from there and see if anyone had seen where they went or if they had any interactions with anyone suspicious.

Jack Dee had been given the task of going through plane and ferry bookings for Sunday. The photographs had been taken somewhere near Belfast but the ransom note had been delivered in London on Sunday night. How had it got there? If that really was the two victims' blood on the page then it couldn't just be a photocopy sent by email to an associate in the capital. It had to be the original page, so someone must have delivered it to London. Who? Perhaps Dee could recognise some familiar name on the lists of travellers. He would go through the security footage from the airports and ferry terminals too. It would be a boring job.

'You sounded like I used to,' Gawn said to Maxwell when they were back in her office.

'Is that a bad thing? I had a good role model, didn't I? You mean, I sounded efficient and authoritative?' he responded with a cheeky grin.

'I was thinking, more, bossy and demanding.'

Maxwell laughed.

'OK. That too. But we need to hit the ground running, don't we?'

'Yes. We need to prioritise the work. If we had unlimited manpower and unlimited time, we could go through everything, but we don't. There's a mound of these videos to watch. They've had their channel for nearly a year and unless we find someone lurking in the background in different locations stalking them, it could yield very little. It could take weeks and I doubt very much we even have days. These kidnappers will be making their demands soon.

'I think it should help to find out more about our victims. Why these two? Norrie, we know a bit about – what his father told me anyway. But Nina seems to be a bit of a mystery. Ambassador Pedersen claimed not to know much about her other than that her parents are dead and she has no family. You'd think she would have been checked out by the Norwegian Security Services if she was living with an ambassador's son.'

'They seem a bit more relaxed about security in Scandinavia,' Maxwell said. 'Their royal families just wander around the streets without a guard.'

'How do you know that?' Gawn asked.

'Kerri's magazines. The wedding of one of the royal family was featured in last month's edition. It was very ordinary. No cathedral and hundreds of guests or anything, and the princess just works in an office.'

'You read your wife's magazines now?'

'I'm a metrosexual in touch with my feminine side. Didn't you realise, boss? I thought Sebastian was too. He's into fashion and cooking and shopping and all that sort of stuff.'

'Right. I believe you, Paul. Sebastian likes fashion and all that sort of stuff as you put it. But if you do, you've changed since I last saw you.' She laughed. 'Anyway, last I heard Kerri does all the cooking and you'd do almost anything to avoid having to go shopping with her.'

'That's only because, when I go, she spends all my money,' Maxwell retorted.

They both laughed. Gawn realised how much she had missed this part of the job. She had missed their easy banter. Maxwell was one of her few real friends. She had always found relationships difficult. She had been let down so many times. He was an exception. They had been through a lot together. They knew the pressures and demands of policing on individuals and on families. She could talk to him in a way she couldn't talk to anyone else, even to Sebastian.

'Right,' Gawn said and straightened up in her chair. 'I think I've put it off long enough. I need to phone the Met. They should have got some results on the ransom note by now. Speaking to Lynch will give me an idea of how much cooperation we're likely to get from them.'

'You think there'll be problems?' he asked.

'I don't know. There shouldn't be. We're all after the same thing, aren't we? But working across jurisdictions is never easy.'

She couldn't help letting a touch of uncertainty sound in her voice.

'Is this some other man from your past, boss?' he asked suspiciously.

Two years ago, he would never have asked her a personal question like this, but their relationship had moved on. If her past affairs with colleagues in the Met were going to impact their investigation, Maxwell had the confidence to ask her directly.

'Yes and no. Matt Lynch was my boss. He was a DCI then. We weren't best buddies. Looking back, I realise I must have been a total nightmare to deal with.'

Maxwell frowned.

Gawn smiled. 'OK. I know I was a nightmare when I arrived here too. You don't need to rub it in, Paul. But I was still recovering when I joined the Met. I'd just left the army. I was readjusting to life in civvy street and I was suffering from PTSD. Not excuses. Just an explanation. If you're asking, did I sleep with him, is he likely to be difficult because he's a spurned lover… then, no, Paul. I didn't sleep with every cop I worked with in London, you know. But Matt's a canny cop and he'll have his own ideas and his own priorities. So long as his ideas don't clash with mine, we'll be fine.'

Chapter 19

'Bloody hell, Gawn Girvin! You're a blast from the past alright.'

Gawn recognised the gruff tones and thick East End accent of Matthew Lynch. There was no mistaking them. He didn't sound angry, more that he was going to enjoy their encounter and make the most of it. His words had exploded in her ear. She remembered he had never needed to raise his voice to get attention in a room because he always spoke at ten decibels higher than anyone else, even in normal conversation.

'Superintendent Lynch,' she said, by way of greeting.

'So, you're a DCI now, eh? Managed not to piss off any senior officers yet or maybe they're more forgiving over in Ireland than we are here?' He snorted.

'Must be. How are you, sir?'

'"Sir", is it? That's not how you used to refer to me if I remember correctly.'

'You weren't a superintendent then and I wasn't a DCI,' she said.

If Maxwell had been in the room, he would have been surprised to see her blush as she remembered exactly what she had called him, even to his face.

'And you didn't need my help then either,' Lynch added.

'True. But we're both dancing to Sir Patrick Montgomery's tune now, aren't we?' Gawn asked.

'Montgomery?'

Gawn knew Lynch was trying to sound as if he had never heard of the man.

'Come on, Matt. He's the one who has your commissioner jumping through hoops.'

'Your chief constable too by the sounds of things,' Lynch said.

'So, let's just do our job and find these kids,' Gawn replied.

'They're hardly kids, Gawn. Norrie Pederson's in his late twenties. He's a post-grad student and the girl's older.'

'You've checked into them?'

'A bit. As much as we could in the time we've had. Norrie seems OK for a rich kid. No red flags. Mr Ambassador was a very successful businessman before he went into diplomacy. There's plenty of money to pay a ransom. Your kidnappers picked well.'

'And the woman?' Gawn asked.

'We haven't got too far with her yet. I didn't want to start contacting the Norwegian police. I thought you might consider it as stepping on your toes, and I know how you'd react to that.' He laughed. 'It is your investigation unless they show up over here or there's more contact from the kidnappers in London.'

'And there hasn't been?'

'Not yet. I have a man with the ambassador. He's shadowing Pedersen and I have a team watching the embassy in case something's left there and we've got permission for a track and trace on their main phone line and Pedersen's mobile if the kidnappers ring with demands.

'The video footage of the note being left under the wipers doesn't tell us much. You'll have seen it by now, I assume.'

'Uh, yeah,' she said.

'Our video analysts are poring over it frame by frame and I have men searching CCTV all around the area to see if they can pick the rider up either on his way to the car or away from it. But they haven't found him yet. He must have ditched the bike so he only had to change his coat and take his baseball cap off to make it hard to recognise him.'

'What about the ransom note?' Gawn asked.

'No fingerprints. I didn't expect any. And it was just ordinary printer paper sold by the thousands of sheets in supermarkets all over the country.'

'What about the two marks on the paper?' Gawn asked.

'You noticed, did you? I thought you might think they were just dirty marks on our photocopier or something.'

She didn't respond to that comment. He knew she wouldn't have thought that.

'Blood. O positive.'

'Both of them?' Gawn asked.

'No. The other was AB positive.'

'Rarer then,' Gawn said.

'Yes.'

'I can get Norrie's blood group from Pedersen's man. He's left one of his staff, a Lukas Dahlstrøm, here in Belfast to act as liaison with the Norwegian police so we get all the cooperation we need,' Gawn told him.

'Very nice,' Lynch said with some scepticism in his voice. 'And to keep an eye on you?'

'That too, I suppose,' she said. 'They'll hardly know Nina's blood group. It might take a bit longer to get that.'

'Our lab wouldn't commit themselves but they implied the O blood was from a male and the AB was female. Something to do with neutrophil appendages. Don't ask me to explain it. I can't. Just more of their mumbo jumbo.'

'One male and one female but no identification yet of which male and which female.' Gawn thought for a moment. 'Thanks, Matt. I need the original note. As soon as possible.'

'Of course. I'll send it over. I'll get one of my men to bring it for chain of custody. I wouldn't want to muck up your case. First flight tomorrow morning suit you?'

'How about this afternoon?'

'I'll see if we can get a flight organised.'

'Thank you.'

Gawn meant it. He had been helpful.

'And if our video people turn anything up or the kidnappers make contact again, I'll let you know.'

'Right away this time, Matt. Not after you've gone over everything yourself.'

'Of course,' Lynch said.

This time Gawn wasn't sure whether to believe him or not. He might be under pressure to pass everything through Montgomery. She knew Montgomery would be breathing down her neck and she imagined it would be the same for Lynch.

Chapter 20

The room was noisy. The whole team had gathered waiting for Gawn to arrive. Even Maxwell was waiting, not wanting to start without her. There were a few nervous faces and at least one officer rechecking her notes.

Gawn walked in. She looked tired. She felt tired. After doing little other than lazing around and being looked after by an over-solicitous husband for almost a year, it had been the mental rather than the physical effort that had taken its toll on her. The sudden call to come in, the meeting in the conference room, the expectations of the anxious father, the presence of the enigmatic Montgomery, coming to terms with the new members of her team and missing those who were no longer there, had all been challenging. Talking to Matthew Lynch had brought back memories too, not all bad.

Gawn positioned herself near the door and nodded to Maxwell giving him a sign to start.

'Right, let's see how much we've learned,' he began.

Gawn feared the answer might be not very much.

'We've been watching their channel,' Jamie Grant began. 'It's quite entertaining. We started with the last one they uploaded. Then began to work backwards. They were at Dunluce Castle and then travelling along the Antrim Coast Road. We could recognise some of the places they were passing. They said they'd picked up a couple of burgers from a drive-thru and then went and parked up in a forest.'

'Which forest?' Gawn asked.

'Don't know, ma'am,' Grant said. 'You see, the videos are all edited. They don't show you everything. One minute they were driving along in the dark, the next they were inside their van with the curtains drawn eating their burgers and talking about what they planned to do the next day. They could have been anywhere.

'Then they did a piece to camera asking for people to click and subscribe to their channel and said their next video would be out in a couple of days. They were going to visit Carrickfergus Castle. That was it. There was nothing unusual. Not that we could see anyway.'

'We watched that last one at least ten times, ma'am,' Sharma assured her. 'Just to make sure we weren't missing anything. No one was following them but we'll have to cross check the time with any traffic cameras in the area to make sure of that. And we don't know exactly when that was yet.'

'We watched a few others too,' Grant said. 'But we didn't see anyone who seemed to be following them or taking a special interest in them. We've a lot more to sit through tomorrow.'

Gawn had watched Grant's face closely.

'Did you have something you wanted to add, Jamie?' she asked.

'I just wondered if maybe they'd managed to attract the wrong sort of attention,' he said.

'Wrong sort?' Maxwell chipped in.

'Well, they're young and good looking. Nina's a bit of a stunner and I think she knows it. She's not afraid to show off quite a bit of her body. She wears these tiny wee tops and hot pants a lot of the time.' Grant made some moves with his hand to illustrate what he meant. Someone giggled. 'They go wild swimming and she wears the tiniest bikini I've ever seen.'

'At this time of year?' Maxwell asked.

'Yeah. I'm sure there must be some of their subscribers who watch to see her like that rather than caring about their travelogues or any cooking tips,' Grant said.

'You think they might have attracted someone who fancied a piece of Nina, Jamie?' Maxwell asked.

'I know that doesn't explain the two of them going missing or the ransom threat but, if someone had grabbed them because they fancied the girl and then found out that Norrie came from money, it might have turned into something more. It could explain why they only sent a photo of the girl. They mightn't have been interested in Norrie at all except for getting a pay-off. They might have got rid of him already. He could be dead.'

Gawn hoped he wasn't right in his assessment of Norrie's condition. But she was impressed. The old Jamie Grant would have sniggered his way through the videos of the girl in the shorts and reported that he'd seen nothing suspicious. This more mature and experienced Grant was using his brains.

From the very beginning she had wondered why the kidnappers had sent a picture of Nina rather than Norrie. He was the one whose parents had the money to pay a ransom. A photo of him, roughed up, would have more chance of getting them what they wanted. As far as they knew, Nina had no money and no family to pay anything and the demand had been sent to Pedersen. Grant could be right.

Chapter 21

'Does anyone have anything to add?' Maxwell asked.

DC Sandra Watt cleared her throat and stood up nervously. Gawn could see a patch of red suffusing the woman's neck and gradually creeping up to her face. Her voice was almost breaking with nerves and she kept glancing between Maxwell and Gawn as if she wasn't sure who she should be addressing.

'I went to Carrick this afternoon and spoke to the staff at three different drive-thru fast-food outlets in the town. No one could remember a fancy painted-up campervan in the last few days but they all have a staff rota. The managers on duty today weren't working over the weekend and it's possible that, when our victims called in, none of today's staff was there either. They've promised to look through the recordings from their pay windows to see if they caught the van on camera.'

'They didn't offer to give you the recordings?' Maxwell asked.

'No, boss,' Watt said and then glanced across at Gawn as if worried the DCI would be offended that she'd called Maxwell 'boss'.

'I didn't push it, sir. If they find something, I'm sure they'll let us know. They were very nice, very helpful.'

'Go back and ask them for the tapes and you can begin going through them yourself,' Gawn said, trying not to sound too critical. 'We don't have the time to wait until they get around to looking. It won't be a priority for them. They'll get busy and forget about it.

'And there's an area for motorhomes in the main car park in Carrick. Up in the corner near the main road. It would probably be a good idea to check that they didn't stop there. They may not have driven through the restaurant at all. They could have parked and walked and they could even have stayed in that car park overnight. Get hold of any footage from the town centre. You'll not be able to get that tonight but start first thing in the morning.'

Gawn noticed puzzled reactions. 'I know they said they went to a forest but remember their footage was edited. It didn't all have to have been taken on the same night. We can't depend on what they say for our timeline. We need to check everything for ourselves. Get hold of that footage, please.' She couldn't remember the woman's first name so finished lamely with, 'DC Watt.' She hoped it didn't sound as if she was annoyed with her. She wasn't. She just wanted to instil some urgency in the team.

Gawn turned her attention to DS Sian Nolan. 'You were trying to find out more about our victims.'

'Yes, ma'am. Finding out about Norrie or rather Norbert Pedersen, to give him his proper name, was easy. Mr Dahlstrøm, the ambassador's assistant, put together a bio for me.'

'The Pedersens don't have any other children. Norrie's twenty-eight. He's a PhD student at the University of Oslo in the Department of Political Science. He dropped out of his course last year, midway through. His father convinced them to hold his place open for him to go back next year. Lukas– Mr Dahlstrøm,' Nolan corrected herself, 'says the ambassador was confident Norrie would get tired of the itinerant lifestyle. He's always loved his creature comforts, according to him.'

'Anything else about him? You've obviously formed a connection with Dahlstrøm. Did you get him to open up with any useful titbits that aren't in any official bio?' Gawn asked.

'He did sort of suggest Norrie might have dabbled a bit with drugs. Not the hard stuff. He was very quick to assure me of that. The Pedersens blame Nina for that and for everything basically. Dahlstrøm thinks it was more likely the other way round. "Norrie is not a saint" was how he put it to me.'

'Good to know but probably worth double checking what Dahlstrøm told you. Don't just take his word for it. Contact the university direct. Get their take on Norrie, talk to some of his tutors if you can, and get the Oslo police to talk to some of his fellow students. And see if Dahlstrøm can give you details about Nina,' Gawn said.

But the sergeant hadn't finished yet.

'I've already tried to find out more about her, ma'am. She's a bit more of an enigma. I questioned Dahlstrøm about her. According to him, she just appeared in Norrie's life. Out of the blue. She was working as a waitress in one of the cafés near the university. Norrie met her and he was besotted with her right away. They moved in together within a week. Apparently, she didn't have anywhere to stay. She'd just been crashing out on friends' couches, sofa surfing.

'She never talked about herself to anyone. If she told Norrie anything, he didn't pass it on. But she has an English accent. You can hear it on the videos. Dahlstrøm suggested she might have been educated in England. Although he doesn't have much of an accent himself. Most Norwegians can speak good English.'

'So basically, you found out nothing useful about Nina?' Gawn asked.

She wasn't exactly surprised or disappointed and she didn't want to sound critical of the sergeant, but Gawn's gut instinct was working overtime. She didn't know what it was about the missing woman but something was telling her that there was something off. The kidnappers seemed to be concentrating on her and Gawn couldn't figure out why. It didn't make sense.

'Not yet, ma'am,' said Nolan. 'I'm still working on it and Dahlstrøm gave me the name of someone to contact in the police in Oslo tomorrow.'

'Do that first thing in the morning, Sergeant.'

Chapter 22

Tuesday

Gawn had spent what was left of Monday evening, after waiting around in the office for any developments, cuddled up in Sebastian's arms in front of a TV programme that neither of them had really been watching. She couldn't relax. She was on edge, waiting for the telephone to ring to tell her the kidnappers had been in touch again.

Seb had cooked dinner earlier so he only had to reheat it when she got home. He'd made her favourite chicken cacciatore with homemade bread. If he had hoped for a night of passion, he was disappointed. She had fallen asleep exhausted before he had made it into bed beside her.

In the morning, she was up and ready to leave before he had surfaced. It was her who brought a cup of coffee to him in bed.

'What time is it?' he asked, rubbing the sleep out of his eyes and sitting up in bed to take the cup from her.

'Nearly six.'

'Six! What are you doing up and dressed?'

He put the cup she had handed him down on his bedside table and patted the bed beside him. She sat down, perching right on the edge of the mattress. He reached out and slowly began to unbutton her shirt.

'You've plenty of time for a bit of fun before you need to leave, babe. There'll be no one else there yet. It's far too early.'

When it seemed she might be going to argue, he added, 'And, if anything had happened overnight, they'd have phoned. You know that. You don't want to let it get too personal, babe. You know how you can get overinvested in your cases. Don't let it get to you.'

He wrinkled his nose up like a naughty schoolboy as he slipped his hand inside her shirt. She didn't try to stop him.

'Come on, my little badass cop,' he said and kissed her throat.

'I need to go, Seb,' Gawn said half-heartedly.

'Five minutes. Come on! Spare a poor guy five minutes, ma'am,' Seb said in a mock cockney accent as he pulled her down on top of him.

'You are such a bad influence on me, Sebastian York,' she said.

'You bet I am and you love me for it.'

* * *

Thirty minutes later, Gawn was straightening her shirt and smoothing her mussed hair back into place in front of the wall of mirrors in their bedroom. She watched Seb's reflection. He was asleep, snoring softly, a smile on his face.

Once in the car, instead of driving along the Marine Highway without stopping, Gawn pulled into the large car park sandwiched between the dominating presence of the Norman castle and a modern supermarket. It was free to use and, during the day, workers as well as shoppers used it, so it was usually busy but it was a little early for most of them just yet.

The Airstream coffee truck which Gawn regularly patronised on her morning runs was just opening up for the day. Gawn watched Diane, the barista, sliding the side shutter open and hanging out a board with the day's specials. She decided not to give in to the temptation of another coffee.

Suddenly a thought came to her. She had suggested to the team that Nina and Norrie might have stopped in this car park to charge up their batteries. Perhaps Diane had seen them. It had only been a guess on her part, just an outside possibility. She could be totally wrong but there weren't many campsites in the Greater Belfast area and, although she knew the pair preferred to wild camp, if they needed to charge their battery, this would have been an easy place to do it.

'Good morning. You're early this morning. No run today?' Diane greeted her with a cheery smile, her eyes taking in Gawn's formal suit.

Gawn had been aware of Diane watching as she walked across from her car. She could tell from the barista's expression that she was surprised to see how she was dressed. She was used to a sweaty runner in tracksuit and trainers. Diane paused with a huge bag of beans in her hand ready to feed the shiny coffee machine. Gawn extracted her new ID from her pocket and watched the woman's eyes widen as she held it up.

'Not coffee you're after this morning then?' Diane asked, her manner still chirpy and friendly despite the early hour and the revelation that Gawn was a police officer.

'No. I'm investigating a missing persons case.'

No need to go into details. Gawn was hoping to keep information about an abduction out of public knowledge and away from the media. Talk of a kidnapping would be front page news and it wouldn't help her investigation. The kidnappers could panic and get rid of their victims. It had happened before. Hopefully they'd get the two back before most people even knew they were missing.

'You didn't happen to see a young couple here in a campervan sometime over the weekend, did you?' Gawn asked.

'This is a really popular spot for overnight stays for motorhomes these days, you know. There's somebody here most mornings when I'm opening up. Sometimes two or three even, in the summertime.'

'You would have noticed these two for sure, Diane. You couldn't miss them. They've painted their van up with cartoon figures.'

Gawn couldn't believe her ears at the woman's next words.

'Oh, you mean Nina and Norrie.'

'You know them?' Gawn asked.

'I don't know them. I've seen them on the internet. My husband and I have a campervan too, you see,' Diane said.

'Did you see them here?'

'Yes. They were here on Friday morning when I arrived. My husband dropped me off on his way into Belfast and he remarked on the van sitting over there.'

Friday. Friday when they were supposed to be at Dunluce. Not Sunday or Saturday which was when they had been searching. Their timeline was wrong. They'd have to start again.

The woman had nodded towards the charging point in the distant corner of the car park.

The ransom note had been delivered in London on Sunday night. If the two Norwegians had been in this car park on Friday morning safe and well, did it mean Pedersen's fears were correct? Could they have set this up to extort money or as a publicity stunt, uploading their earlier footage and muddying the timeline to let them get away somewhere and hide themselves and the van?

'You didn't speak to them, did you?'

'No. In fact, come to think of it, I didn't even see them. Only the van. It was there and then I got very busy. I'd intended to go over when I got the chance and introduce myself, tell them how much I enjoyed watching them, but the next time I got a minute to draw breath, the van was gone. Friday is my busiest day.'

'Did you see them leave?' Gawn asked.

'No.'

'What time did you notice the van was gone?' Gawn asked.

'Some time after the lunchtime rush. Maybe about two o'clock,' Diane said but her expression suggested she was guessing.

'Thank you. That's really helpful,' Gawn said. 'And I'll take an espresso now.'

She thought she might need it.

Chapter 23

There was a new spring in her step as Gawn headed along the corridor to Maxwell's office. It was in a corner of the incident room where he could oversee what was going on. She wanted to tell him what she had found out from Diane. They would need to widen their parameters on all the CCTV searches.

As she made her way across the office, through the ranks of desks, Maxwell came out to meet her.

'Have you heard the news, boss?' he asked before she had the chance to speak.

It couldn't be anything about the kidnappers making contact again. She had left explicit orders she was to be phoned if that happened, no matter what time it was – day or night. She wasn't really in the mood to play twenty questions with him.

'No. Why? What's happened?' she asked, walking past him into his office and removing her jacket, putting it over the back of his spare chair. She began rolling up her sleeves. 'Something to do with our two missing Norwegians, I hope. Have they turned up?'

'No. Nothing about them. Denton Fraser was found dead yesterday.'

He waited for her reaction. He knew she would have one. She sat down on his spare chair and blew out her lips in a soundless whistle.

Gawn had always thought Denton Edgar Fraser, to give him his full name, had been born to be a lawyer with a name like his. He already sounded like a whole law firm just on his own. In fact, he was one third of one of the largest local firms of solicitors, Fraser, Torrens and McMurray or FTM according to their logo. He specialised in criminal law and was well-known to the criminal fraternity. He was well-known to the police as well and she had come up against some of his clients before. It was a running joke among officers that 'Call for Denton!' was the most often-heard refrain in the holding cells and interview rooms of the city's police stations.

'Was it a heart attack?' she asked, only slightly interested.

The last time she had seen him, in the halls of the High Court over a year ago, his complexion had been unhealthily florid, the result of high blood pressure, she had supposed.

'Try again,' Maxwell said. Something about his tone and the look on his face made her think it was not a natural death.

'An accident?'

No reaction.

'A robbery gone wrong or something?'

Fraser would have expected to have immunity from burglary because of his known associates. No one in their right mind would have dared break into his home or office. He knew too much and he knew too many dangerous people.

55

'I don't have all the details yet. But when control got the call to his house yesterday morning, the first responders found something that made them involve Serious Crime pronto. Organised Crime's there now too. Read into that what you want. Sam's SIO.'

Gawn wondered if Maxwell was disappointed not to be leading that investigation rather than playing second fiddle to her.

The 'Sam' he had named was DI Samantha Rainey who had once worked on Gawn's team. The two women had started out wary of each other but ended up as friends of a kind, or as close to a friend as Gawn was with any of her female colleagues.

'Good luck to her,' Gawn said. 'Some villains will be heartbroken to have lost their ace card.' There was no doubt Fraser had been good at what he did.

'Now, let's forget about Fraser. He's got nothing to do with our two Norwegians. I have important news for you.' Gawn explained how they had a definite sighting of the campervan in Carrickfergus on Friday morning.

'That gives us something to work with at least. We should be able to get CCTV and traffic camera footage from Thursday and Friday and see what happened to them,' Maxwell said.

'I just wonder if someone's been messing with the timeline deliberately to make finding them more difficult,' Gawn said.

'The kidnappers?' Maxwell asked.

'Would they have the technical knowledge to do that? What about Norrie? He could do it easily.'

Maxwell's phone rang, interrupting their discussion. He picked up the receiver and listened carefully. Gawn couldn't make out what the voice on the other end of the phone was saying but she quickly realised it concerned her.

'She's here with me now … Right, I'll tell her.' Maxwell turned to Gawn. 'Aoife McWilliams wants to see you,' he said.

'Aoife McWilliams?'

Gawn didn't recognise the name.

'Right. Of course. I forgot. She's new since your time,' Maxwell said.

Gawn thought that made it sound like she was some retiree who had called in to see him for old time's sake and been out of the job for years. She'd only been gone for twelve months.

'She's with Strategic Communications and Engagement. It's something about the News and Media Desk.'

Gawn rolled her eyes. Journalists were not her favourite people.

Chapter 24

'You see, Gawn, we really need to get ahead of this story. We need to take control of the narrative. Otherwise someone will get hold of it and it will blow up in our faces. Why didn't we say anything? Why were we keeping it secret? We'll have conspiracy theorists crawling out of the woodwork.'

Gawn was in a small office with a view straight onto a high brick wall. It was neat. There seemed to be a place for everything, and it was brightly decorated with a row of what looked like family photographs on the shelf of a bookcase of colour-coordinated lever arch files. A pretty little girl in a party dress with blond curly hair and braces on her teeth and twin boys in school uniform smiled at her from across the room. She'd never set eyes on the woman lecturing her before, but she'd had plenty of time to wonder what she was going to be told as she'd made the short journey to Police HQ. As she listened to McWilliams trying to sound convincing, she thought that some of the conspiracy theorists mightn't be so far wrong.

Aoife McWilliams was the epitome of elegance and grace. She had stood up from her desk when Gawn arrived. The DCI had been surprised to be face-to-face with a tall blonde. She was used to being the tallest woman in any room but McWilliams was almost as tall. Gawn had glanced down and saw the woman favoured high heels too. She recognised Louboutins when she saw them.

McWilliams' long blond hair hung loosely over her shoulders but somehow she managed to make it look controlled not untidy. Her big brown eyes could have given her a soulful appearance but she seemed cheery and friendly and her welcoming handshake had been firm. Gawn's first impressions had been favourable, not what she had expected at all. She had little time for courting the press.

McWilliams' words however were much less welcome.

'I got a call from a journalist friend of mine last night.'

Journalists were only friendly when they wanted something, Gawn had always found. She didn't respond to the comment. She waited to hear what the call had been about and what it meant for her. That was, after all, why she was here.

'There are rumours doing the rounds in Belfast. Nothing more than that at the minute, my friend said. But some noises about a kidnapping. She was obviously hoping I would confirm it and offer her an exclusive.

'I think we need to pre-empt any speculation by issuing an appeal through our social media channels about your two missing Norwegians. I know, before you say anything' – McWilliams held up her hands as if to physically prevent the DCI speaking – 'that the normal procedure is to wait to issue a public appeal unless there are compelling concerns. I know the procedure. Normally we would only circulate a covert briefing to our local safeguarding partners at this stage but you're not sure yet exactly where these two went missing, so who do we brief?'

It sounded like an accusation to Gawn and she didn't have an answer.

'And under normal circumstances these two wouldn't be regarded as vulnerable per se so we'd wait before going public to see if they turned up, but they are high profile and there have been some cases of missing persons in the last year, while you've been away, turning up murdered. That's caused a lot of criticism and the suggestion has been we didn't react quickly or decisively enough.'

'So, it's not normal circumstances this time,' Gawn interjected.

'Got it in one, Chief Inspector.'

So, they were *her* missing Norwegians now, Gawn thought to herself. And if they didn't turn up or, if they turned up dead, it would be down to her, nothing to do with delays getting the information to her or the games she thought might be being played in circles far above her head.

'What do you intend to say in this press release?' Gawn asked.

'Standard stuff. I'll draft it. You'll be named as heading the investigation.'

'Won't that alert the press that it's a bit more than just a couple of missing persons we'd like the public's help to locate? It wouldn't be usual for a DCI from Serious Crime to be involved. The journalists will know that,' Gawn said.

Any journalist who was anyway good at their job would have more questions after a press release like that with her name in it, she thought. She knew the press office released this type of appeal frequently. It seemed ever more frequently as people were choosing to disappear for a myriad of reasons. Mostly they turned up again safe and sound within days. But sometimes they didn't and it could be months before a body was found.

'I intend to drop some hints to a few friendly journalists that you're being eased back into the job on health grounds after your career break. That's why you're working a low-key missing persons case rather than your usual murder cases,' McWilliams said.

Great, Gawn thought to herself. They're going to present me as some charity case detective on her last legs.

'Do you really think anyone will buy that?' Gawn asked.

Unfortunately, even as she asked, she thought they might. Her last case had been tough and walking away for a year suggested she'd had problems afterwards. She hadn't had a breakdown but she could have. Seb had got her through it.

McWilliams locked eyes with her. 'Cards on the table, Gawn?'

Gawn didn't know this woman. Until twenty minutes ago, she'd never even heard of or set eyes on her. She knew nothing about her and she certainly didn't know if she could trust her. Everyone, even inside her own organisation, seemed to have their own agenda.

'This is going to hit the press sooner or later', McWilliams continued. 'You know it and I know it. And, when it does, it will be a major story. I'm simply trying to control the narrative. That's all. We don't want to start off on the back foot.

'I'd intended we'd start low-key with the normal kind of appeal on our social pages, maybe a short mention on radio and TV if they pick it up. All that kind of thing. It would have helped to find them if they've just taken themselves off grid for a couple of days. It's worked in other cases.'

The press officer paused and Gawn waited.

'I'm not telling you this, OK?'

McWilliams didn't speak until Gawn had nodded her agreement.

'There's been a bit of pressure to mention your name specifically.'

McWilliams couldn't fail to notice Gawn's reaction.

'Someone wants my name out there?'

'So it seems. You're to be the public face of the investigation. For whatever reason, someone wants everyone to know you're involved.'

'Why me?' Gawn asked but she knew McWilliams wouldn't know the answer to that. 'Who?'

'I'm not sure. It's just a word here, a suggestion there. When I got the call from my friend, she just said an anonymous source had contacted her and mentioned your name in connection with it so we couldn't hide your involvement even if we wanted to. What I'm suggesting is a sort of damage limitation for you.'

Gawn didn't know whether to believe her. If McWilliams felt under pressure, she would know or at least suspect who was behind it. But Gawn didn't think it was worth trying to add to that pressure to get a name. Even if she got one, it probably wouldn't be the right one. It would be someone who was being manipulated. That was exactly how Gawn had been feeling since the start of the case.

'I'll draft a standard appeal. I'll mention your name but try to bury it down at the bottom somewhere. If you're lucky no one will notice. That's all I can do at the minute, but I wanted you to have a heads-up. Once someone does pick up on it, the press will probably start digging and you can expect them on your doorstep.'

Gawn thanked her. She wasn't exactly sure what for. She supposed it was better to be aware of the coming storm. It wouldn't change how she went about her work. She stood up, ready to leave.

'There is one saving grace in all this,' McWilliams said.

'What's that?'

'Denton Fraser getting himself killed. They'll all be busy with that for a while.'

Gawn had never expected to be grateful to the slippery old solicitor.

Chapter 25

Although she wouldn't have admitted it to anyone, Gawn's conversation with McWilliams had unsettled her. Something was going on. There were forces pulling strings.

Lukas Dahlstrøm, Pedersen's PA, was staying at a hotel in the hills overlooking Belfast. As DCI it was her job to keep an overview of the case. She didn't need to do everything herself; as Maxwell had reminded her, he was perfectly capable of running the team. He had already passed on the information about the new timeline and restarted the searches.

As SIO, she should be the one liaising with Pedersen's representative. She could just phone him but she was glad of the excuse to get out of the office and have time to think after what she'd just heard. It was only a twenty-minute drive from Brooklyn House through the countryside of North Down to his hotel. Within minutes of driving under the barrier at Police HQ, she was in the hills above Belfast, drumlin country, her car window down to let in a rush of fresh spring air.

Ostensibly the purpose of her visit was to inform Dahlstrøm of the public appeal which was going to be issued and to warn him to prepare himself and the ambassador for a coming news scrummage when, not if, journalists began poking around. No matter how banally McWilliams might try to word it, once mention was made of missing tourists and her name, someone was bound to pick up on it. It was just a question of how quickly they would connect Nina and Norrie, and the questions would start.

Really, she was making the journey because she wanted the chance to talk to the Norwegian herself. She was sure Nolan had asked all the right questions, but nothing was as useful as hearing a witness's comments for yourself and watching their face as they answered.

'Coffee or tea, Chief Inspector?' Dahlstrøm asked with impeccable manners.

Gawn declined his offer. Nolan was right. It would be hard to identify Dahlstrøm as Norwegian from his accent. If anything, he sounded slightly American and there were even touches of a Northern Ireland intonation in his speech. Perhaps he was one of those people who picked up local accents wherever they went.

'I wanted to come myself to thank you for the help you've already given my sergeant,' Gawn said by way of introduction.

'My pleasure. It's always good to be of assistance to a pretty woman.' Dahlstrøm inclined his head towards her.

'And I wanted to warn you that our press people are issuing an appeal for the public's help in finding Nina and Norrie. Today. It's what we normally do in missing persons cases. We've found social media to be a very useful tool, and with Nina and Norrie being well-known on the internet and their shenanigans appealing to the sort of age group that engages with social media rather than the traditional media, we could get some useful information.'

Dahlstrøm raised his eyebrows at her in a sightly supercilious look.

'Their what?' he asked and took a sip of his tea.

'Shenanigans,' Gawn repeated. 'You don't know the word?'

Dahlstrøm nodded.

'It means, well, silly behaviour, I suppose. It's what my old granny used to say about some of the things I got up to when I was a child.'

'Shenanigans. Yes. I like it. Very appropriate.'

Dahlstrøm smiled. Gawn wondered if there was a touch of disdain in his manner. He worked for Pedersen. He wasn't a friend of Norrie's. At least, she didn't think so.

'How well do you know Nina and Norrie, sir?' she asked.

'Please, let's dispense with the "sir". Call me Lukas. Nina, I don't know so well. I only met her after Norrie had invited her to move in with him and he brought her to meet his parents. But Norrie I've known for some time. As Mr Pedersen's personal assistant, I'm not embassy staff. I have accommodation in the Pedersen's home.'

He took another sip of his tea.

'Were you surprised when he went off with Nina in the campervan?'

'Maybe. A little. I knew he was head over heels in love with her. He worshiped the ground she walked on.'

Gawn noticed Dahlstrøm's use of the past tense when talking about Norrie and wondered if it meant anything.

'And what do you think of Nina?' Gawn asked.

She was beginning to wish she had taken Dahlstrøm up on his offer of coffee.

'She's very pretty. Very lively. Sexy, I suppose, if you like the sort of woman who likes to jerk men around.'

'Does Nina like to do that?'

'I think so,' the Norwegian said guardedly.

'Did she try to jerk you around?'

Dahlstrøm laughed.

'I'm much too old for her, Chief Inspector. Old enough to be her father. She knew she'd be wasting her time with me.

'She likes to use people, I think. She used Norrie. He had great prospects before he met her. His father would have set him up in business or even in a career in politics. He could have done anything he liked. Instead, he was living in that little van, moving around, mixing with all sorts.'

Past tense again, she noted.

'He preferred to chase after her. He threw it all away.'

Dahlstrøm sounded more like a disappointed lover than an employee to her.

'I've heard he dabbled with drugs,' Gawn said.

'I imagine that was down to her as well. He'd smoked a bit of weed as a teenager. Nothing stronger until she introduced him to cocaine.'

This man wouldn't be joining Nina's fan club any time soon. That was clear.

Chapter 26

Nina was surprised to see the other man bringing her some food this time. It was usually the one who had cut her arm; the one who sneezed all the time; the one whose eyes drilled into her, enjoying the depths of anguish he was seeing there; enjoying her suffering.

'Here you are, love. You need to keep your strength up.'

This man's voice was not so harsh. And his movements were not so rough as he took her hands in his and cut the plastic bindings holding them tightly together. She was so weak her hands fell down onto her knees like two lead weights. She could barely hold them up. The blood coursing back into them was painful too. She whimpered. The man reached out and she drew back sharply, fearing another blow. Instead, he had run his hand over her head. His touch was almost comforting.

'Hush. I'm not going to harm you, love.'

When he held out a mug to her, she couldn't take it from him. She knew she would drop it. He held it to her lips and let her sip the warming liquid.

'It's only soup, love. Not poison, you know.'

Not today it wasn't. But some day it would be. Or, if not poison, then that knife again.

For all this man's gentler manner, she knew they were going to kill her. She just didn't know when.

Chapter 27

It was mentioned almost at the end of the local lunchtime news bulletin. At least it wasn't the main story, Gawn consoled herself.

> *Police in Mid and East Antrim District Command are becoming increasingly concerned for the welfare of two Norwegian tourists who have been travelling around the province in a campervan.*
>
> *Nina Larsen and Norbert Pedersen were last seen in the Portrush area on Wednesday, March 6 and were known to be intending to travel along the Coast Road to Carrickfergus.*
>
> *DCI Gawn Girvin, who is leading the search team, said, 'Nina Larson is 5'4" tall. When last seen she was wearing a plain white T-shirt and blue shorts with a white stripe. Her companion, Norbert Pedersen, is 5'11" and of slim build. He was also casually dressed in blue jeans and a T-shirt with "San Diego" on it.'*
>
> *Officers ask the pair, or anyone who saw them on the Coast Road or who was in the Carrickfergus area on Friday and noticed anyone matching Nina's and Norbert's description, to contact them at Carrickfergus station on 101, quoting reference number 179906/03/24.*

Gawn's name was in the centre of the report, easily missed. At least, that was Gawn's hope. As she thought about the rush to issue the appeal, she wondered if this was someone's idea of an ass-covering exercise in case the couple turned up dead. Then the top brass could claim they had been looking for them right away without causing too much of a fuss and embarrassing the ambassador, but deploying a senior detective to lead the search.

As she listened, Gawn realised she was learning two new pieces of information. Firstly, someone had found the girl's second name. She was Nina Larsen, and secondly, that Norrie's name was a diminutive for Norbert. Even some of their biggest fans might not recognise them from those names. She hoped.

Chapter 28

Back at Castlereagh, Gawn visited the toilets before going to her office. She thought she had the place to herself, but when she came out of the cubicle, she saw the back of a woman clutching one of the hand basins. She was bowing over it so Gawn couldn't see her face in the mirror, only the top of her head. But she saw the woman's shoulders moving slightly as if she was crying.

At the noise of Gawn's footsteps behind her, the figure straightened and looked up and Gawn immediately recognised Sam Rainey in the mirror. Rainey swung round and a smile replaced the look of despair Gawn had seen for an instant.

'Gawn! I'd heard you were back.'

She seemed embarrassed to have been caught like this but there was no hesitation in the greeting as there had been with Maxwell. Rainey stepped forward and hugged her briefly, both aware someone could walk in on them at any second.

'I hear congratulations are in order,' Gawn said, washing her hands.

Now she could see Rainey's face more clearly, Gawn was sure she had been crying.

'Are you alright?' Gawn asked.

'Sure. Of course. Why wouldn't I be?' Rainey sniffed. 'I'm the lucky bitch who got a high-profile murder case to investigate. Haven't you heard? This could make my career, according to the chatter.'

'Someone's been giving you a hard time,' Gawn said. She wiped her hands on a paper towel and discarded it into an already almost overflowing bin.

She wasn't asking a question. Rainey's uncle had been an assistant chief constable although he had moved on to Police Scotland. Even before she had met Rainey, Gawn had heard the gossip about nepotism. Once she had worked with her, she'd quickly realised the woman had earned her promotions but that didn't make any difference to some people.

'Not to my face, of course. But you see the looks. You hear the whispered comments. Just never quite loud enough to be certain of what you heard so you can challenge them.'

Gawn patted Rainey's arm in an awkward attempt to show support.

'Just do a good job – which I'm sure you will – and the bastards can keep their comments and their thoughts to themselves. This place is no different to anywhere else, Sam. You know that. We have to work twice as hard to be considered half as good.

'I guess the super is one of the ones on your back,' Gawn said.

'No. He's off on long-term sick.'

This must be one of the gaps Wilkinson had mentioned, Gawn supposed.

'I'm meant to report to the chief super, but he only wants to know if we make a breakthrough. He says he's too busy for the minutiae of an investigation. It means he's standing back waiting for me to fall flat on my face.' Rainey shrugged.

'I know you won't have got too far yet. It's early days. But I'd be happy to hear any updates whenever you can. Later today, if you like. No pressure. At least it will give you the chance to talk it over with someone who's on your side. Then they can bitch about both of us.' Gawn laughed.

Didn't she have enough on her plate without mentoring Rainey? Probably. But she couldn't stand back and not help her friend.

Chapter 29

The incident room looked and sounded busy with a buzz of chatter as people talked on the phone or pored over reports together. Gawn was impressed. It felt good to have a team working like this. Maxwell had been doing a good job while she was away. She'd have to be careful to give him the space and responsibility his rank deserved. She mustn't fall into the trap of treating him like her sergeant again. And she knew she'd been guilty in the past of trying to do too much herself and rushing off following her hunches.

Maxwell walked across to her brandishing an A4 sheet of paper in his hand. She immediately thought of the ransom note and wondered if there'd been another.

'They've had some calls already in response to the media appeal,' he said and glanced down at the page. 'Carrick is dealing with them. A bit of triaging to help us out. They'll weed out the known cranks. If they think anything is worth following up, they'll let us know.'

'We've got the girl's full name now I see,' Gawn said.

'Yeah. Sian's been in touch with Oslo. Sian,' he called across to the sergeant.

Nolan eased herself out of her seat and walked briskly across the room, her heels tapping out a quick rhythm.

'Yes, sir?'

'How did your chat with the Norwegian police go?' Gawn asked.

'It went well, ma'am,' Nolan answered turning to face the DCI. 'I spoke to an Inspector Busch from Kripos. Did you know they have a reindeer police unit?'

'Somebody has to make sure Santa obeys the traffic laws on Christmas Eve, Sian. We wouldn't want a sleigh crash with all the presents. Think of all the disappointed kids,' Maxwell joked.

Nolan laughed.

Gawn could see that Maxwell had managed to create a much more relaxed atmosphere in her absence. It seemed to work.

'What's Kripos?' Maxwell asked, suddenly serious again.

'It's their National Criminal Investigation Service, sir,' Nolan said. 'It specialises in organised and serious crime. It's their hub for international police cooperation too.'

'I've been at their headquarters in Bryn,' Gawn said. Her voice told them she wanted them to move on.

'Busch says Nina's last name is Larsen. At least that's what the people at the café where she was working told him. But she was only filling in extra shifts, off the books, so they didn't have any documentation for her. And she doesn't have a passport and Busch says they can't trace her anywhere. They don't know where she was born or where she went to school. She just seemed to turn up in Oslo out of nowhere. He assured me they'd go on looking and see what they could find. He promised to be in touch again today after he's made some more inquiries.'

Back in Maxwell's office, the two began to discuss the state of the case.

'So, we have a Norwegian man, Norrie Pedersen, whose father thinks either he or his girlfriend could be behind the whole kidnapping, and we have a mystery woman, Nina Larsen, who just appeared out of nowhere. Pedersen said he thought her parents were dead but he suspected she had criminal friends and drug connections. That might just be wishful thinking because he obviously doesn't like the girl. Dahlstrøm seemed to confirm that to me although he didn't offer any proof. Busch needs to be following up on that too. Maybe I should talk to him myself.'

'It's one of the hardest things I've had to learn,' Maxwell said.

Gawn shot him a puzzled look.

'What is?' she asked.

'Delegating. You can't do everything yourself. Sian is a competent officer. And she's good with people. She'll have chatted Busch up big time and she'll keep at him until he comes up with the goods. I don't think it would be a good look for you or for her to be tramping all over her work. Let her do her job. You do yours,' Maxwell said.

'Which is what?' Gawn asked.

'You're the boss. You can't micromanage every detail, or question every suspect yourself. You can't chase after every lead like you used to do. You need to have the overview. Trust your team. I do.'

Gawn thought for a minute.

'I trust you,' she said.

'Well, that's a start. Now—'

Before Maxwell could finish his sentence, Nolan was at his door.

'Sorry to interrupt, ma'am, sir, but I thought you'd like to know, Inspector Busch has been on with me again.

They've had a breakthrough. They established when Nina arrived in Oslo and they got her passport details. Larsen isn't her real name. She's Eileen Deeley. And she's not Norwegian at all, she's British.'

'Eileen Deeley,' Gawn said, tapping her index finger on her lips. 'Deeley. Does that name ring any bells with you, Paul?'

'I don't think I've ever heard of anyone called Deeley. Except that TV presenter woman. Sian, run it through the UK database. If she changed her name, it might be because she has a police record,' Maxwell suggested. 'The hints we were getting about drug connections might be right.'

'She had a passport,' Gawn said. 'Get someone to contact the passport office and get their records. We need her address. Maybe her parents aren't dead at all. I don't think anything will surprise me about this woman.'

Chapter 30

Gawn was standing in her office poring over an Ordnance Survey map of County Antrim which she had spread out on her desk. She knew the area well. She could picture the route the two would have driven in their campervan.

If they wanted lots of beautiful scenery to show their followers and to provide photographs for the book they were supposed to be writing, then they would have followed the coast road down through a string of quaint little seaside towns. Cushendun, with its caves; Cushendall, overlooked by the flat-topped Lurigethan Mountain. It had a lovely beach where she could remember playing as a child. She was just speculating if they might have stopped off at Glenariff and if it could be the forest where they had talked about filming, when there was a knock at her door.

'Come.'

'I've got the details Inspector Maxwell said you wanted, ma'am.'

It was Nolan. The woman seemed slightly wary of her, barely venturing into the room, hanging back at the doorway and Gawn wondered if she had been too sharp with her earlier.

Nolan moved forward and held the page out to her.

'Just tell me, Sergeant. I don't need to read it.'

'Eileen Deeley gave an address in Liverpool on her passport application. I looked it up and did a search on the internet to see what it's like. It's an expensive-looking property. Big, detached house. I checked on the electoral register. The house is owned by a Mr Gerald Deeley. He owns an auction house in central Liverpool. I think I might have seen him on one of those antiques programmes on TV. And Eileen's on the register too along with a Mrs Marie Deeley, presumably her mother.'

'We need confirmation that this really is the Nina we're looking for. She could have stolen someone else's identity to get a passport. Contact Merseyside police and ask if they'll send someone out with a photograph of our missing woman and get a confirmed ID for us, please.'

'On it, ma'am.'

Nolan seemed relieved to get away.

Progress of sorts. She knew Carrick police were chasing up all the sightings that had been phoned in. Maybe something definite would turn up there. But what they really needed was for the kidnappers to contact them again. What were they waiting for?

Chapter 31

She was so weak. She could hardly lift her head and she felt so tired. She had taken the soup but now she thought it might have been drugged. She was disorientated, drifting in and out of consciousness.

'There we go, princess.'

She hadn't heard the sneezing man coming back. She wondered how long he had been there, just watching. Now he was propping her up against the wall and holding a cup of water to her mouth. She slurped it up, almost choking on the liquid. It felt icy cold as it dribbled out of the sides of her mouth and down her chin. She licked her lips.

'Have to have you looking your best, don't we, princess, for your starring role?' He laughed. 'You know all about camera angles and flashing your tits to get clicks.' This time he laughed even louder. It was a cruel laugh.

The man put his hands either side of her throat and, for a second, she thought he was going to strangle her. This was it. This was how it was going to end. Instead, his rough fingers moved down to the neckline of her T-shirt and ripped the flimsy material apart, revealing her bra. Then she saw the knife. Was he going to cut her again? She pushed back into the wall as far away from him as she could get. But there was no way she could escape him. If he was going to hurt her or kill her now, there was nothing she could do about it. She was powerless.

She remembered the words of a child's prayer she had said by her bedside every night when she was very little. Her father had knelt beside her and they had intoned the words together, their little nightly ritual as he put her to bed. She began to say them.

'Now I lay me down to sleep, I pray the Lord my soul to–'

'No. No. No, princess. You're not going to sleep. I need you wide awake.'

He slapped her across the face, but not too hard. She was jerked up onto her feet and dragged across to a chair. It was only then she noticed the second man was there too. She was facing him but she could only see his eyes.

The sneezing man thrust a piece of paper into her hand. 'When I tell you to, read what's on this paper. Nothing else. No tricks. Otherwise, I'll kill you.'

She had no doubt he would. Maybe death would be preferable to this uncertainty. It was going to be her ultimate fate anyway. They weren't going to just let her go, were they?

She felt the man move in behind her, his hands pressing down on her shoulders, his fingers digging into her skin to position her on the chair. She saw a camera sitting on a tabletop tripod, just like the setup she and Norrie used.

'Read it. Now.'

The red light on the camera started blinking. She hadn't spoken for so long, she wasn't sure what her voice would sound like. The first few words sounded strange, almost strangled, as she forced them out.

'We want the photograph we sent published in the papers. We want to see it on TV too. Show the photograph. Let everyone know we mean business.'

Nina knew she had been kidnapped. They would kill her but perhaps this would buy her some more time.

'We want one million pounds' worth of uncut diamonds,' she read, not believing the words as they came out of her mouth. One million!

Her words were stilted. The man's fingers pressed harder into her shoulders. One million pounds. Did Norrie's father have that kind of money just lying around?

'That's our price. You have three days. After that, the price goes up fifty thousand every day and you'll get back… one piece less every day.'

Her voice had finally faltered until she felt the sharp point of the knife touch the back of her neck. She flinched and read on.

'Three days. Friday. We'll be in touch with the details of where and when.'

Nina screamed. And screamed.

Chapter 32

Gawn's watch vibrated on her wrist, buzzing like an angry bee against her skin. Sebastian knew it was to be used only for emergencies during working hours.

Why would he be calling her? He knew she was in the middle of an investigation.

'What is it, Seb?' she asked, not even trying to hide her irritation.

She heard his unsteady breathing and knew there was something wrong. Something serious.

'I have something I think is meant for you,' Seb said.

'What do you mean you have something meant for me?'

'What do you think I mean?' he snapped back at her. 'Sorry, babe. Listen. I was out shopping. I wanted to go to the community greengrocer to pick up some fresh vegetables for tonight's dinner.'

'Yes. I get it, Seb. I understand. But what happened? Did someone give you something for me?' she asked.

'Nobody gave me anything.' He paused and she heard him taking a deep breath before going on. 'I emptied out the last of the fruit and veg and got to the bottom of the bag just a couple of minutes ago, and there was something there. Something I didn't buy.'

'Dear God, what was it?' she asked afraid of what the answer might be.

'An SD card.'

She exhaled slowly, relieved it was nothing gruesome. She knew she had enemies and some of them had twisted minds. With her name appearing in the press at lunchtime, one of them might have decided to send her a welcome home present. She'd imagined a dead rat or a photograph of her with some threatening message.

'And it's for me? How do you know it's for me?' she asked.

'I didn't at first. I thought it was just a mistake. It was just an SD card. I thought maybe it had dropped into my bag by accident. I remember setting my bag down a few times when I was paying in different shops and when I was in for coffee, it was sitting out beside my table.' Seb was gabbling now.

'Did you touch the card?' she asked, her mind in overdrive.

'Of course I touched it. I didn't think it was going to bite me or blow up or anything. It's just an SD card for God's sake.'

Just an SD card? Why was he so upset if it was just an SD card?

'OK. So, what makes you think it's for me? Maybe somebody did just drop it into your bag by mistake when you were queuing up.'

'I put it into my computer to look at the photos on it, Gawn. I thought I might recognise somebody local in them and then I'd be able to return it. I thought it was probably someone's happy holiday photos or maybe wedding pictures or something.'

He was gabbling again, and his voice was shaking. She could imagine his pale face as she listened.

'Take it easy, honey. What's on it? What did you see?' Gawn prompted gently.

'It's some poor girl, Gawn.'

He didn't need to go on. Gawn realised who it would be.

'A picture of her?'

'A video.'

'Have you watched it?' Gawn asked.

'Only the start. That was enough. I was too afraid of what might happen to her at the end.'

So was Gawn.

'I'll send someone to pick it up from you. It'll probably be Jamie Grant. You know him,' Gawn said.

'Of course, I do.'

'Don't watch any more of it, Seb.'

'Don't worry. I won't.' He sounded very definite. 'Gawn, is this the case Wilkinson needed you for? Is some poor girl being held and tortured?'

The hairs on Gawn's neck stood on end at the word.

'You know I can't tell you, Seb.'

'I saw her. I need to know, Gawn.' He was speaking so quietly she could hardly make out what he was saying.

'Yes. I think so.'

'Then I'm glad it's you who's looking for her.'

Chapter 33

Gawn's mind was full of speculation about what was on the SD card and why the kidnappers had chosen to slip it to Sebastian. Why him? It meant they must have been watching him. Been close to him. Very close. She didn't like that thought, and she blamed Aoife McWilliams. She had put Gawn's name in the press release. The woman hadn't had any choice; that must be how the kidnappers had known about her involvement.

A confident knock on the door distracted her from her anxieties.

'Come.'

It was Rainey. She looked tired but more composed than she had earlier. Gawn had almost forgotten she had told the DI to come with an update on the Fraser murder. She had only done it to have the chance to offer some encouragement. She had every confidence in Rainey doing a good job.

'Is this a good time, ma'am?'

'As good as any, and skip the "ma'am", when there's no one else here. Sit down, Sam. How's the case going? Have you established that it's murder? Fraser didn't happen to develop a sudden conscience and commit suicide, for example?'

'Not unless he could shoot himself in the back of the head. Twice. The boys who were first on the scene checked his vital signs but he was already dead. Stone cold. He'd been dead for some time. Two bullets.'

'Two taps,' Gawn said. 'A professional job.'

'There was very little blood and no exit wounds, so the first responders weren't sure of COD because they didn't move the body to see the wound on the back of his head. They thought he might have fallen and just hit it. But the room was a mess and they recognised Fraser, so they called it in. Jenny was able to confirm it was murder after ten seconds.'

Jenny was Dr Jennifer Norris, the pathologist. She was Gawn's friend and Gawn had thought, before she had left for California, that Jenny and Sam might have begun a relationship but she had heard nothing more about it.

'You said the room was a mess. Anything taken? Do you think it was a break-in gone wrong?'

'It wasn't a break-in, Gawn. There was no sign of forced entry. Whoever killed him, Fraser let him in.'

'Someone he knew then,' Gawn said.

'Yes. As you'd expect with somebody like Fraser, there were lots of security cameras all over the place but the ones inside the house were switched off. He probably only used them when he was out or during the night. His clients wouldn't be too keen on being filmed.' She laughed. 'We did catch someone arriving on the doorbell camera. That's how we know Fraser let him in. But the shooter kept his head turned away so we have no visuals of his face.'

Rainey sighed.

'Well, at least it gives you a time of death which Jenny will be able to confirm at the PM. When do you think he was killed?' Gawn asked, her professional curiosity kicking in.

'Late on Friday night.'

'Friday?' Gawn said surprised.

'He lived alone. His housekeeper doesn't work at the weekends. She saw him on Friday afternoon. We can't find anyone who saw him alive after that. She found him dead on Monday morning when she arrived for work. Friday is also when the camera shows someone at the door.'

'Do you know what was taken; what they might have been after?' Gawn asked.

'I asked Mrs Ritchie, the housekeeper, to have a look around and see if she noticed anything missing. She said maybe some files. But she wasn't sure. The filing cabinet was lying open and files were scattered all over the floor. Some could be missing. She says she has no way of knowing. The cabinet was always locked when she cleaned his study. She wasn't allowed to touch it.

'The doorbell camera caught the perp arriving and leaving. He could have had files hidden inside his jacket. The only other thing missing for sure is Fraser's Rolex.'

'What about forensics?' Gawn asked.

'They've been working at the house since yesterday. I'm waiting to hear what they find. I'm sure some of Fraser's more heavyweight clients might have come to the house to see him privately rather than going to his office, which means the CSIs might find a lot of interesting fingerprints but not necessarily anything to connect anyone directly to the murder. Mrs Ritchie cleaned the room on Friday morning so, if she's dusted well, there mightn't be too many old prints.

'Fraser was semi-retired. I've checked with his office, but they didn't think he was handling any special clients at the minute. He'd been diagnosed with high blood pressure and he was winding his work down. He was going to retire to his villa in Spain, according to his secretary.'

'What about CCTV from the road outside his house?' Gawn said.

'The shooter didn't arrive by car. At least not at the front of the house. He walked along the street so we're trying to trace his route from private security cameras and traffic cams, but you know how much time that takes and how easy it is to miss something. It was dark, and the quality of a lot of the recordings isn't that great.

'They're trying to pick up his trail but some of the street cameras aren't even working. Funding cuts,' Rainey explained and rolled her eyes. 'So, it's a waiting game at the minute. A bit like yourself. You're waiting to hear from the kidnappers again, I take it?'

'I think we just have, Sam. Grant's gone to collect it. An SD card.'

'Maybe you'll have a quicker answer than me then.' Rainey smiled ruefully.

'Thanks, Sam. Keep me informed and, if anyone gives you any aggro, let me know. But I think you can fight your own battles.'

Rainey had almost reached the door when she turned and said, 'It's a bit of a novelty to have a boss you feel is actually on your side instead of waiting for you to trip up.'

She walked out closing the door behind her.

Gawn wondered if she could say that about her own boss. She wasn't thinking about Wilkinson.

Chapter 34

'It looks... so bloomin' small and ordinary, ma'am, doesn't it?' Grant said as he offered Gawn the tiny SD card inside an evidence bag on his open palm.

'What did you expect, Jamie? That it would be covered in blood or have a skull and crossbones on it?'

'No, of course not, ma'am.' Grant laughed. 'But it's lucky Dr York even noticed it, isn't it? He could have missed it. It could have lain at the bottom of his bag for ages.'

Gawn didn't want to contemplate that. If Seb hadn't noticed it or had thrown it away, or even handed it in to lost property at the council offices, they'd never had got the message, at least not in time, and Nina and Norrie could have been killed. Thank goodness he'd found it and decided to check it out, even though that meant more trouble for her. Now that he knew the kind of people she was dealing with, he would be fussing around her again.

'Get it fingerprinted. Seb will have handled it,' Gawn said and frowned.

Grant interrupted her.

'I thought of that, ma'am. I took his fingerprints at your house for elimination purposes.'

'Good work, Jamie.'

She was impressed he had thought to do that. He looked pleased.

'Get it straight to Tech Support, before we're tempted to start messing around with it ourselves – just in case we destroy something. Seb's already opened it and I'm sure the kidnappers want us to see what's on it but I'm not taking any chances. This is our link to the victims and to them. We need to know what they want and we need the experts to give us any other information they can get from it.

'Gee them up, Jamie. Make sure they know how time-critical this is. And don't let them fob you off with any excuses about first thing tomorrow morning. I know it must be the end of their shift and they'll be itching to get home. Tell them I'll approve any overtime.'

She didn't know if she could do that, but she was doing it anyway.

Grant was about to leave when her next words stopped him.

'How was my husband when you saw him?'

Gawn felt awkward asking. She had always kept her home life with Sebastian separate from her work life. She never talked about 'my husband' to the team. Most of them knew very little about him other than he was a successful writer, and very few had met him. Grant had, years ago when she had first met him during a case.

'He seemed a bit shook up, ma'am. He was having a brandy to steady his nerves when I left.'

Grant smiled. Gawn smiled back at him. She wasn't surprised to hear this.

'Thank you, Jamie. Now, tell them to put a rush on this. I want to see whatever's on here within the next thirty minutes. No longer.'

She felt a little better now.

Seb wrote crime novels about a female police detective and she'd watched crime movies with him, some of them quite graphic, but that was just make-believe; you knew it was actors and make-up.

This was real life.

Chapter 35

'Ready?' Gawn asked.

They had got back to her in under fifteen minutes. They were probably keen to get home and must have dealt with the card right away. Her email had pinged and, when she saw the message was from Tech Support with an attachment, she had phoned Maxwell and asked him to come to her office. She didn't want to watch it alone.

Gawn wiped her hands down the front of her trouser legs. They still felt damp. Maxwell had carried his chair round to her side of the desk and sat down beside her in front of her computer screen.

'Did they get any useful information from the card?' he asked.

'Not yet. According to the email the geotag has been tampered with. They'll keep working on it.'

'OK. All we need now is some popcorn,' he said but his expression didn't match his jokey words. 'Sorry. I'm just trying to lighten the mood a bit.'

Maxwell had been trying to sound blasé but Gawn knew him well enough to know he was feeling as tense as she was. She remembered watching an old home movie with him of a girl being gang raped as part of a cold case they'd investigated together. He'd had nightmares after it, he'd told her. So had she.

'Go for it,' she ordered.

She closed her eyes for a second as Maxwell clicked the mouse to open the folder.

The girl who appeared, filling the screen, was recognisable as the same girl from the photograph the kidnappers had sent to Pedersen. Nina Larsen or Eileen

Deeley. Gawn still thought of her as Nina. But she was barely recognisable as the laughing, flirty girl from the internet videos Grant and Sharma had been watching. This girl's hair was wild, uncombed and matted. Her face was streaked with tear tracks.

There was an ugly purple mark on her cheek which must have come from a blow. Her T-shirt was ripped open revealing her skimpy bra, which had once been pink but now looked grubby and stained.

For ten seconds the figure was totally still. No movement. No sound. Gawn could almost believe it was just an effigy she was watching. That is, if you didn't look into the woman's eyes and read what they were saying. They told a story. Nina was terrified. Her chest started heaving up and down as she gulped for air. Gawn recognised the symptoms of a panic attack. Nina began blinking rapidly. She raised her head to look directly into the camera and marks could be seen on her throat. Marks left by fingers. She had begun shaking so much, she looked in danger of falling off her chair.

A man's figure moved into view behind her but he could only be seen from the waist down. He was dressed in black jeans. There was a threatening darkness all around him.

Nina raised a piece of paper into view in her shaking hands. The fluttering of the paper was caught by the microphone and sounded like a flock of birds in flight. Her voice, when she started to read, sounded as if every word was an effort.

'We want the photograph we sent published in the papers. We want to see it on TV too. Show the photograph. Let everyone know we mean business.'

Nina sucked in a lungful of air and closed her eyes for an instant as if she was hoping this was all a bad dream and she could wake up. She opened them and began reading again.

'We want one million pounds' worth of uncut diamonds.'

Gawn and Maxwell looked at each other.

'That's our price. You have three days. After that the price goes up fifty thousand every day and you'll get back... one piece less every day.'

Nina's voice faltered. Nina hesitated for longer than before and, in response, part of a man's hand came into view and his fingers pressed down hard on her shoulder. Gawn felt Maxwell move in his seat beside her, his knee knocking against hers as he leaned in closer to the screen. Nina glanced up at the figure whose face was out of shot and started reading again immediately.

The message was not finished yet. Nina flinched again and jerked her head forward. A knife could be seen at the back of her neck, the pointed blade just touching her skin.

'Three days. Friday. We'll be in touch with the details of where and when.'

Nina finished reading and dropped the page as if it was on fire. It floated down out of sight.

A man's hand, with a heavy gold signet ring on the little finger, reached around over Nina's body. The hand was gripping a knife with a serrated blade. His other hand was still firmly on her shoulder stopping her from moving, pinning her down on the chair. Gawn caught a glimpse of what looked like an expensive watch on his wrist. Nina didn't look as if she could have moved. She was frozen to the spot in terror. Without warning, the knife sliced into her body just above her right breast. She screamed, an echoing sound which seemed to go on forever. Blood gushed from the wound down over her breast. The screaming continued until the screen went blank.

Chapter 36

There was a stunned silence in the room. If Gawn had had a clock in her office, they could have heard the ticking. But she had no clock so the silence was intense, unbroken.

'The bastards. They really mean business, don't they?' Maxwell almost breathed the words at her. His face was white. She had watched as the colour had drained from it. 'They're not fooling around, are they?'

'Did you ever think they were, Paul?' Gawn said, standing up and moving across to her filing cabinet.

A cafetière was sitting out on a tray on top of it. Steam was curling up to the ceiling like a smoke signal in an old western movie and the familiar aroma of her favourite strong blend filled the room as she pushed the plunger down.

She didn't really feel like drinking coffee but she needed to be doing something after what they had just witnessed and she was glad to be able to have her back turned to Maxwell so he couldn't see her face. She was sure she must look as pale as he did. She had seen sights as bad as this, and worse, especially in Afghanistan, but her year away from the job had helped her forget the depths of cruelty and inhumanity that were out there under a thin veneer of civilisation.

'Do you think they cut her breast off?' Maxwell asked and looked up at her.

'God, no, Paul. They'll keep her alive until they get what they want.'

Her voice almost sounded convincing, but she wasn't fooling herself and she didn't really think she had fooled him either.

'I guess it's obvious that Nina and Norrie aren't involved. If it is just a set-up, Nina certainly isn't in on it. She could have been made-up in that first photograph,' Maxwell suggested, 'couldn't she? But she wasn't acting this time.'

'Mr Suspicious,' Gawn responded with a sardonic smile.

'Accept nothing. Question everything. Isn't that what you always told me, boss?'

Maxwell was beginning to sound more like his usual self. They were both struggling to find some sense of professional detachment and equilibrium in the face of what they'd just witnessed.

'Yes. I did. It's a lesson worth learning. I don't think we can take anything at face value on this case. Not what we're being told by Pedersen and Montgomery, maybe not even what we're seeing. Nothing. We need to verify everything for ourselves.'

She held out an empty cup to him. 'Fancy a coffee?' The mug shook slightly in her hand.

'No.'

Gawn poured herself a cup. She sat down again beside him, but set the mug down on her desk, untouched.

'I really did suspect that it was a scam at first, you know,' she said. 'I thought Nina and Norrie could have set it all up to get some money from his father or maybe to get publicity for their channel. I mean, can you imagine what the press would make of this, Paul? Their downloads would go viral. They'd make a fortune from – what do they call it – clicks?

'But it must be genuine. At least I think it's genuine about Nina. Those two photographs could have been doctored, but what's just happened... what we just watched... how she was cut, that was real. She wasn't faking it. She was terrified. But did you notice, Paul, there was no mention of Norrie.'

'So, it is still possible he could be involved? Could the figure with the knife be Norrie?' Maxwell said slowly.

'Anything's possible. But why would Norrie or these kidnappers, whoever they are, ask for payment in diamonds?' Gawn asked. 'Wouldn't they want cash? Diamonds, well, you'd need contacts to get rid of uncut diamonds. It wouldn't be straightforward, and you'd not get the full value when you sold them on.

'But, if it is real, then there's another question, Paul. If someone with connections in London was going to grab them, why do it here? It would be so much easier to grab them somewhere on the mainland. You'd need to have somewhere to hide them and their van.'

'So, you think it's locals now?' Maxwell asked.

'I don't know what to think, Paul. But they're being held here, if those photos weren't doctored to show the cranes. I suppose we have to consider that, although I imagine Montgomery and the experts at the Met will already have confirmed that by now. But someone from the gang was definitely here to slip the SD card into Sebastian's bag.'

'Could it be an OCG,' he asked, 'looking for an easy source of money?'

'Maybe. But diamonds wouldn't be an easy source, would they? I suppose we'd better get on to Maitland. See what he has to say.'

DCI Davy Maitland was her counterpart in the Organised Crime team. 'We'll need to see if he's got any intel or if he can suggest anyone we should be looking at.'

'Leave that to me, boss. Davy and I are in the same golf club. I'm quite friendly with him.'

Gawn stared at her inspector.

'I didn't know you played golf, Paul.'

In fact, she had thought she knew he didn't. They'd even joked about it in the past.

'Took it up while you were away, didn't I? Kerri bought me a set of clubs for my birthday. She thought it would be a good move to help me to make contacts. She was right.'

Maxwell must have noticed the expression on Gawn's face for he hurried on.

'What about weirdos who chanced on the vlogs? We mustn't forget Jamie's suggestion that there could be a sexual element to it. I think our knifeman was getting his jollies there,' Maxwell said. 'Did you hear his breathing?'

She had, and she had noticed the ring on his finger.

'We'll need to try to trace that ring he was wearing. It wasn't engraved but there might be some way to find out where it came from and who bought it.'

Gawn knew that was a long shot and would take a lot of time, time they didn't have.

Maxwell was still sitting in front of the computer and he turned sightly in his seat to get a better view of her face.

'It just seems too well organised for me to be some random pervert who liked what he saw and decided to have a piece,' she said. 'It's a gang. Remember, we've already decided there must be at least two or three of them working together.'

Gawn paused for a moment and absentmindedly took a sip of her coffee.

'Could it be some group operating on the dark web?' Maxwell asked.

'I suppose we should check with Human Trafficking. See if they know of any group like that. And someone will need to check for any punters with a known predilection for using a knife on their victims.

'What I don't understand, Paul, is, if they're just planning to rape Nina, why torture her on camera for our benefit? They could be selling that sort of footage on the dark web. But if it is really a kidnapping, why aren't they showing us Norrie beaten up if they're really after money from his father? Why isn't it Norrie appealing for the ransom to be paid? It's his dad who has the wherewithal to pay them. Why are the kidnappers concentrating on Nina and showing us what they're doing to her?' Gawn asked. 'We need to find her.'

She banged her fist down hard on her desk almost spilling the rest of her coffee. She hadn't really been asking Maxwell. She was talking to herself.

Chapter 37

After the filming was stopped Nina found herself lying on the floor semi-conscious but aware of a burning pain in her chest. At first, she had thought she was dying. Then, as the pain got worse, she wished she was.

She became aware that her two captors were arguing. She concentrated on that, listening to what they were saying, to take her mind off the pain. She didn't open her eyes. She kept them tightly shut, clenching her teeth together and trying to pretend even to herself that she wasn't really there; that this wasn't really happening.

But she listened. Carefully. She had already given her two captors nicknames. It had been her attempt to humanise them, in the hope that she might be able to win them over and escape. Somehow.

The man who had just cut her, she had dubbed 'Sneezy', like one of the seven dwarfs from the old fairy tale. There was often a dark side to fairy tales. The other man she had called "Doc". He seemed to be the boss. He wasn't around so much. He didn't do so much of the menial fetching and carrying, bringing her food or supervising her toileting, and he had shown some kindness when he was feeding her the soup.

'What the hell did you do that for? Are you trying to frickin' kill her? The boss will go crazy if anything happens to her before he gets what he wants. He'll blame us,' Doc said.

Doc sounded scared. Nina was surprised. He wasn't the boss. There was someone else behind this; someone even scarier if Doc's reaction was anything to go by.

'Lighten up, for God's sake. It's not a deep cut. It's nearly stopped bleeding already. I'll clean it and patch her up. Don't worry. She'll be fine.'

'Huh!' Doc didn't sound convinced.

'Look, that will have them sitting up paying attention. A wee bit of blood works wonders, you know. Pedersen and Girvin will be pissing themselves now. They'll believe us. And he'll pay up. No problem. And it'll get the message through to–'

'OK, OK. Maybe you're right,' Doc interrupted him.

Nina wondered who Girvin was. She didn't know the name.

Sneezy seemed to have finished speaking and Doc wasn't putting up any other argument. Nina was about to open her eyes when Sneezy spoke again.

'Anyway, I enjoyed doing it. Cutting her. Knives and guns are my thing. The boss knows that. If we have to send a few pieces of her back, he knows I'll do the job.' He laughed, long and loud.

Nina held her eyes tight shut, wishing she had not heard his words. A shiver ran down her spine.

Chapter 38

It was a difficult phone call. She had known it would be. She could have gone to the hotel and told Dahlstrøm or just phoned him and let him contact Pedersen with the ransom demand. But that wasn't in her nature. She didn't dodge difficult jobs.

'Chief Inspector?'

Pedersen sounded tense. There had been only a short delay after she had spoken to an assistant explaining who she was and asking to speak with him. He had obviously left instructions he was to be told immediately if she phoned. He was probably hoping for some good news.

'Mr Pedersen, I have news– not bad,' she added hastily.

She could hear the slow release of the ambassador's breath down the phone.

'I thought…' He didn't finish his sentence.

'We haven't found them yet, but the kidnappers have made contact again and we know what their demands are now.'

'Did they send another photograph? Did Norrie look alright?'

'They sent a video clip this time but Norrie wasn't in it,' Gawn said to pre-empt any more questions. She wasn't going to tell him about Nina's condition.

'We're complying with everything they've asked. They've no reason to hurt him. And we do have definite lines of inquiry we're following.'

She was trying to sound upbeat and positive. How could anyone be 'alright' being kidnapped? If they were treating Nina like this, what could they be doing to Norrie? If he wasn't involved, of course.

'What do they want?' Pedersen said, suddenly sounding business-like.

'They want a million pounds worth of uncut diamonds by Friday.'

Gawn expected disbelief and protestations of the impossibility of getting the ransom. She expected him to quibble at the amount or question how he was supposed to get diamonds so quickly.

'I can manage that.'

She wanted to ask him how but, before she could, he offered her an answer.

'My wife is Dutch, you see, Chief Inspector.' He said it as if that should explain everything. 'Her family has extensive interests in the diamond business in Antwerp. I have investments in the company. I can call in some favours to get hold of the diamonds quickly. They will cooperate. I can arrange to fly in to hand them over.'

'The kidnappers said they'll contact us again with details about delivering the ransom. They may ask that you do it or they might just want it left somewhere. In which case one of my officers can do it. That would be safer. As soon as we hear the arrangements, I'll contact you again. Please let me know when you have the diamonds ready.'

He rang off. She knew he would be glad to have something to do. Waiting was always the hardest part.

But their conversation had raised yet more questions for Gawn. Asking for diamonds had seemed a strange request. For most people it would have been difficult, even impossible. But not for Pedersen, it seemed. Had the gang done their homework before kidnapping the pair or had Norrie offered the information?

Chapter 39

Wednesday

Maxwell was on the first plane out of Belfast to Liverpool on Wednesday morning. He'd already spoken to DI Starr from Merseyside Police late on Tuesday evening. The Englishman had confirmed Nina's identity as Eileen Deeley and agreed to break the news to her family that the PSNI believed she had been kidnapped. He promised to send a Family Liaison Officer to stay with them and to get a trace on their phones in case the kidnappers contacted them.

Now Starr was driving Maxwell to the family home.

'Nice area,' the Ulsterman said, looking out of the car window at the passing view.

Maxwell didn't like lengthy silences with strangers. They made him uncomfortable. Starr had seemed friendly enough when he'd picked him up at Liverpool John Lennon Airport but Maxwell was acutely aware that they needed local cooperation, and he felt under pressure too. Having Gawn back in charge was a challenge. Wilkinson had given him free rein to run his own investigations. He'd enjoyed that. He wondered how long it would be before Gawn was involving herself more and more, and he wanted to come back from Liverpool with something useful.

Starr didn't reply to Maxwell's casual comment. It had been a stupid thing to say anyway. What did Maxwell know? He was a stranger here. He'd only been in the city once before with some mates for a football match and he couldn't remember much about it. It had been a good weekend.

Eventually they had left the city centre behind and were passing through the outer suburbs, big houses with two or three fancy cars in every driveway. The Deeleys did have money, Maxwell thought to himself. Maybe not as much as Pedersen but the kidnappers might try extorting money from Nina's family too.

Starr made a sharp turn into one of the paved driveways and brought his car to a smooth halt behind a shiny red Jaguar. The two men walked up to the front door which was opened as they approached. A pretty blonde dressed casually in jeans and a sweater stood there. She had been watching out for them.

'Morning, sir,' she said to Starr. She sounded too chirpy for Maxwell's liking.

'DC Ingram,' Starr said, indicating to Maxwell that this was the FLO.

Ingram led them through a wide hallway into a bright, airy kitchen at the back of the house overlooking a massive lawn with a pergola and a barbeque area at the far end. Maxwell couldn't help thinking the whole place was like something from one of the magazines Kerri liked to buy. A middle-aged man and woman were sitting either side of a glass-topped table. A steaming mug of something sat in front of an empty chrome and black leather chair. The FLO must have been sitting there with them.

There was what Maxwell interpreted as a strained silence between the parents or perhaps it was just the prospect of getting some more bad news from him. Mrs Deeley was clutching a mug with an incongruous yellow smiley face on it. Her eyes were red and her face anything but smiley. A box of paper hankies sat out on the table in front of her, already opened and half empty.

The couple had looked up as the two men walked in. They recognised Starr. He did the introductions.

'Mr Deeley, Mrs Deeley, this is Detective Inspector Maxwell from Belfast. He's investigating your daughter's... disappearance.'

Maxwell took a step closer to the table. He was watching the couple carefully. First impressions were always important in an investigation, not just with suspects, and they could be revealing.

Starr had told him at the airport that the Deeleys had been shocked at his news. They had been away on a mini-break to Venice, including a trip on the Orient Express, and hadn't received any ransom demands.

They had been blissfully unaware that anything was going on. Sometimes their phone signal had been poor and since learning what had happened to their daughter, Mrs Deeley had been almost hysterical at the thought that she might have been trying to contact them for help but hadn't been able to get through.

But there had been nothing in the mail which had accumulated while they'd been away. Mr Deeley had checked his emails too and they had no messages on their house phone or missed calls from numbers they didn't recognise. The kidnappers must be focusing their demands on Pedersen.

Gawn had taught Maxwell to make his own judgements about witnesses and suspects. Nothing should be taken at face value. Everything should be questioned until it could be verified. Sometimes what wasn't said could be as important as what was and sometimes a look or a gesture, no matter how fleeting, could reveal a lot.

What Maxwell was seeing was a distraught mother. Marie Deeley looked as if she had simply thrown some clothes on randomly to be ready for his arrival and whatever might happen today. Her bright pink jumper clashed violently with her red trousers. There was a stain on the front of the trousers where she had spilled something, probably tea. He guessed under normal circumstances she would have rushed to change. But these weren't normal circumstances. She was wearing no make-up and the wrinkles around her throat confirmed her fifty-five years. Her hair was held back in a rubber band, and, as he watched, her hand shook as she set her mug down on the table.

Gerald Deeley was a different matter. The word 'dapper' came into Maxwell's mind. Navy trousers, sky blue shirt, bow tie and yellow-checked waistcoat instantly reminded the detective that he had seen this man before on television. He was the antiques expert Maxwell and Kerri had watched talking knowledgeably about Georgian silver and glassware. Maxwell noticed the man had taken time to shave carefully that morning and the smell of his expensive cologne reached the detective's nostrils. But he wouldn't jump to any conclusions about Deeley's relationship with his daughter. People reacted differently in situations of stress. Where Mrs Deeley looked as if she was falling to pieces, her husband appeared overly calm, almost detached. Perhaps he had taken something to help him.

'Thank you for talking to me,' Maxwell began. 'I know this must be a very difficult time for you.'

He was deliberately keeping his voice low and even. He didn't want to encourage them to react emotionally. He'd get more from them if he kept them calm. But, if neither Nina nor the kidnappers had been in touch with them, there might be little they could tell him to help trace the pair.

'You had no idea at all that Eileen was missing?' he asked, remembering to call their victim by her real name and shaking his head in what he hoped was a sympathetic manner. He was sympathetic. Although his children were younger, as a parent he could understand how these two were feeling.

Marie Deeley sniffed and blew her nose loudly into one of the paper hankies which she had taken from the opened box.

'Eileen has gone her own way for a long time, Inspector,' Gerald Deeley said. 'We'd got used to not hearing from her for months on end. She likes to think she's very independent. We knew she'd get in touch whenever she needed something from us. Like when she'd run out of money again.'

Maxwell detected more than a touch of bitterness in the man's words. He was surprised. Or maybe he wasn't. Was this another case of spoilt little rich girl going off to rebel, knowing the safety blanket of daddy's money was there to catch her when she fell?

'Now, you know she always remembered my birthday, Gerry,' his wife contradicted him, placing her hand over his in a gesture of familiarity but maybe also of gentle rebuke.

The mother was Eileen's defender, it seemed; the father was more critical. Maxwell had come across this sort of situation before. A mother who could see no wrong in her offspring but a father who understood what their child was really like. He would try to get the chance to talk to the parents separately. He would learn more that way.

At the sound of Marie Deeley's voice, Maxwell had reacted. Not at the words. The husband was a Liverpudlian. Through and through. His accent left no doubt of that. But Marie was from Northern Ireland. There could be no doubt of that either. She had a broad Belfast accent Maxwell couldn't mistake.

'You're from Belfast?' Maxwell said without thinking.

'You'd think I'd have lost my accent by now, wouldn't you, Inspector? I haven't been back in nearly thirty years.'

The smile on her face was a sad one.

Maxwell waited for more information. Silences were important. Gawn had taught him that. Witnesses often felt the need to fill the void and you could learn important facts without having to ask anything.

'My husband and I moved here when Eileen was just a wee tot. She was only about three, nearly four at the time.' Marie had looked to her husband for confirmation. He nodded.

Maxwell's inquisitive gaze turned to Gerald.

'Not me, Inspector,' the man said, as if keen to distance himself from any Belfast connection. 'I didn't meet Marie until after her divorce.'

Maxwell swivelled back to look at Marie. She lowered her head under his gaze. Then she looked up and he was struck by the stunningly violet eyes which met his stare. He could almost imagine the pain she was feeling.

'I was married before. My first husband, Alan, and I moved here in 1995.'

'So, you're not Eileen's father, sir?'

Maxwell had turned his gaze back to Gerald, keen to maintain eye contact with both parents as they answered his questions.

'No,' he admitted with an expression which Maxwell interpreted as reluctance or maybe relief. 'I adopted Eileen officially after we got married.' Gerald looked across at his wife and she smiled weakly back at him. He reached out and patted her hand for just a moment. 'I'm a good father. I've always provided for her. I didn't treat her any differently to the others when they came along.'

Maxwell knew from Nolan's inquiries that Eileen had a brother and sister. At least he had thought he knew. Now he realised they were a half brother and sister.

'Where are your other children at the minute?' Maxwell asked. He looked around almost as if he expected them to appear. Shouldn't they be here to support their parents?

'Katie works in America. She has a job in New York,' Marie said with obvious pride, 'and Damien is taking a gap year before university. He's travelling around Europe on a student railway pass. Last we heard he was in Poland. We haven't told either of them yet about Eileen. They'll be devastated.'

Chapter 40

Maxwell, Starr and Marie Deeley were sitting on uncomfortable rattan armchairs in an overheated conservatory under a laden sky. Gerald Deeley had mentioned an important business meeting and Maxwell had jumped on the comment and encouraged him to go.

He'd had a quick chat with the father in the hallway of the house before he left. Gerald had made it clear Eileen had been a handful. Once she'd gone to university, she'd changed. From being a 'sweet wee thing' as a child, she'd decided to 'run with a bad crowd'. He'd had to pay off debts she'd run up. He thought it was most likely for drugs but he hadn't asked. He just wanted to shield his wife from any trouble. Marie thought the "sun shone out of Eileen's arse". He didn't need to tell Maxwell that he didn't share that view.

'She's been nothing but trouble over the last couple of years,' Gerald had finished.

Maxwell wondered what had happened to the woman over the past two years. Was it just bad influences?

He had wanted to get the opportunity to talk to Nina's mother on her own too. He still thought of the woman as Nina. Marie Deeley's link to Belfast couldn't be a coincidence.

'I suppose it's a bit of a stupid question, Mrs Deeley, asking why you and your husband decided to leave Belfast in the 1990s and set up home in Liverpool,' Maxwell began.

He didn't remember the Troubles, but he'd watched a film with Kerri about a young family fleeing Belfast for a better life. He would probably have done the same for his family if he'd been in that situation.

'You'll not remember what it was like, Inspector. You're far too young,' Marie answered and smiled sadly at him. 'I can hardly remember it myself. It's more like a bad dream now.

'But, even during the worst of it, it was still always home. It wasn't all bad, you know. We had a nice house. Not big' – she allowed her eyes to look around the conservatory – 'but comfortable. My husband had a good job. We had plenty of friends. My parents were still alive then. We'd never even considered moving anywhere else although some of our neighbours had emigrated to Australia and Canada and sent photos back of their new houses and big cars.'

She stopped to take a sip of her tea.

'What changed?' Maxwell asked.

'I don't know,' Marie said, slowly shaking her head. 'I didn't then either. It happened so suddenly. Alan just came home one night in a terrible state and said we were leaving.

We left the next day with only a couple of suitcases between us.'

She looked from Maxwell to Starr and back again as if they might be able to provide an answer for her.

'There were all sorts of terrible things happening then, you know. You learned not to question things too closely. I didn't even ask Alan why we needed to go. I trusted him. I just thought he'd been warned off or threatened or something. Or maybe someone was trying to get him involved in something. He was never interested in any of that. Later, I tried to ask him but he wouldn't tell me.'

She took another sip of her tea.

'You're sure your husband wasn't involved in something with the paramilitaries?' Maxwell asked.

'Something?'

'He wasn't a member of one of the organisations or maybe of a gang?'

Maxwell didn't elaborate. Marie Deeley knew exactly what he meant.

'No. Nothing like that. Alan worked hard. He loved me and Eileen. He spent his free time in the evenings doing DIY. He wanted to sell the house when he had it done up, and for us to move somewhere bigger outside Belfast and maybe have more kids. He wasn't involved in anything.'

Marie took another sip of her tea and Maxwell waited again. He caught Starr, in the corner of his eye, fidgeting in his seat. The local man was obviously keen to ask a question. Maxwell hoped he wouldn't. Marie was talking. She would tell them more if they didn't interrupt.

'But he changed after we came here, to Liverpool.' Marie's voice dropped, as she was remembering that time. 'At first, I thought it was just because it was all so new and so different. We were both homesick, for our families, for Belfast – Troubles and all.' She laughed. 'We had no proper home and no friends. He didn't even have a job for the first few weeks although Alan didn't seem short of money. Then he got a job in a warehouse, which was not what he'd been used to.'

'What did your husband work at in Belfast?' Maxwell asked.

'He was an engineer,' she told them with a touch of pride in her voice. 'He had qualifications. He'd been to college. He worked in an engineering company. He could have done well. Here, he was working nightshifts in a warehouse driving a forklift. Unskilled work. All he needed was a driving licence. He was barely making the minimum wage. He hated it.

'I thought it was all the changes that were getting him down. He was depressed. He started drinking too much. He got…' She hesitated and Maxwell sensed her reluctance to go on.

'He got?' Maxwell prompted.

'He got violent sometimes,' she said.

'With you?' Maxwell asked.

'Sometimes,' she admitted. 'But he was always so sorry afterwards, Inspector.'

'With Eileen too?' Maxwell pressed.

'No.' Marie Deeley feigned outrage but Maxwell wasn't buying it. He waited silently.

'Alan worshipped the ground she walked on. But one night he snapped. He hit her. Just the once. Not hard. She wasn't really hurt. We didn't have to take her to hospital or anything, or go to see a doctor. It hardly even left a mark. She could have got as bad a bump just falling out in the street playing. But it nearly killed him. He couldn't forgive himself. He left the next morning. I never saw him again. I don't even know if he's dead or alive.'

Chapter 41

'The case of the disappearing father,' Grant said melodramatically and waved his arms in the air like some Victorian music hall compère. The others all laughed. 'Are we adding that now to our investigation, sir?' he asked Maxwell with a cheeky grin on his face.

The team was packed into the incident room. Maxwell had begun the briefing, giving details of his trip to Liverpool. He had already reported to Gawn. She hadn't joined them yet but, as the laughter was just dying down, she walked in. One look at her face was enough to bring instant silence. She was in a bad mood. She had an urgent appointment with Wilkinson and McWilliams about releasing the photograph of Nina and, as she'd told Maxwell, she was expecting an argument with them.

'Can I share the joke?' she asked sharply.

'Sorry, ma'am,' Grant said and looked down at his desk.

Gawn took a deep breath. 'No. I'm sorry, Jamie. I know everybody's working flat out on this one. Sometimes I just let things get to me too much. A bit of humour helps, doesn't it? Go on, Inspector. Don't let me interrupt.'

Maxwell looked surprised at her apology.

'You're right, Jamie. We do need to find this missing father now too. If he's alive. DI Starr's team has started looking in Liverpool. So, let's see if we can beat them to this Alan Phillips, eh? I want a complete background check done on him from the day he was born. No matter what Mrs Deeley says, he must have been up to something so serious he had to uproot his family overnight like that. We need to find out what it was.

'And I need you' – he was looking at Sharma now – 'to start analysing that video we got from the kidnappers last night. See what you can spot that we might have missed.' He looked across at Gawn including her in his comment.

'Already on it, sir,' Sharma said and from the look that passed between him and Maxwell, it was clear that the detective constable had already seen the video.

As Maxwell had been speaking, he had been pinning a photograph up on the board.

'Who's that, sir?' Watt asked.

'That's Alan Phillips. Nina's real father. It's an old photo. Taken in 1995 just before they left Belfast. Mrs Deeley provided it. It's the last she has of him. He probably looks very different now. If he's still alive.'

Grant had stood up and was staring at the photograph.

'I've seen him somewhere,' he said slowly.

'Where?' Gawn and Maxwell said in unison.

'I think it must have been in one of the vlogs.'

Sharma had swung round at his desk and was staring closely at the board too.

'Was he following them? Did they meet him somewhere?' Maxwell asked.

'No. It was…' Sharma swung back to his computer and his fingers flew across the keyboard. 'Here.'

He cast his screen to a large monitor on the wall. Nina and Norrie's vlog started playing. Nina was standing at the sink in their campervan. They could see her mouth moving but the volume was turned off.

'What are we meant to be seeing?' Gawn asked.

'Wait,' Sharma said and then paused the video. 'There. On the fridge behind her.'

Everyone could see a coloured photograph of Nina and a man standing outside what was instantly recognisable as the General Post Office in Dublin. The picture was held in place by a magnet from Dublin Zoo. The man was Alan Phillips. There was little doubt. He looked older. His hair was not so thick nor so dark. His face looked more lived-in, but he had the same smiling eyes which he shared with his daughter. His arm was round her shoulder and she was gazing up at him adoringly.

'Where was she when she had the photo up there?' Maxwell asked quickly.

'That's the vlog from Derry at the beginning of last week,' Sharma answered.

Maxwell turned to Gawn.

'What does it mean?' he asked.

Gawn could see pieces of a jigsaw puzzle slipping into place in her mind. She thought she was beginning to understand but she wasn't going to commit herself. Not yet. And not in front of everyone.

'We need that background check on this man. Today. Not tomorrow. Now where are we on the CCTV search for the van?' she asked.

'We spotted the van in the car park alright. It was right up in the corner. But we couldn't see anyone around it except the man driving it away,' Nolan said.

'Norrie?' Gawn asked.

'No, ma'am. Too big and too tall.'

Gawn wasn't surprised. She was convinced now that neither Nina nor Norrie were involved in this, other than as victims.

'Have you run facial rec on it?' Gawn asked.

'We couldn't get a good enough look at his face. He was wearing a baseball cap and a hoodie. He kept his head down the whole time. I've sent it to Tech to see if there's any chance his face was reflected in the wing mirror on the campervan. All it looks like to us is a blur but they might be able to get more with all the programs and equipment they have. And I wondered if it was worthwhile issuing an appeal for any dashboard footage anybody might have,' the sergeant suggested.

'Good idea, Sian,' Gawn said and smiled at the young officer.

Chapter 42

The solid oak door to Wilkinson's office was right in front of her but Gawn hadn't knocked on it yet. She was taking a beat to gather herself. The noise of some men who had just turned the corner into the corridor and were making their way towards her, made her act.

'Come in.'

When Gawn walked into the room, she saw the back of McWilliams' head. The woman was sitting in a chair across the desk from the ACC. Wilkinson was in her usual position but Gawn was surprised to see a pair of spectacles perched on the end of her nose. That was a new development. It made her look rather bookish, like some forgetful academic. Gawn felt as if she was back at school and being called to the headmistress's study.

'Take a seat, Chief Inspector,' Wilkinson ordered.

No first names. No offer of coffee today. Straight to business.

'As you obviously know, the kidnappers want the photograph of Nina Larsen—'

'Eileen Deeley or Eileen Phillips actually,' Gawn interrupted her and saw the puzzled look that appeared on Wilkinson's face.

'We've identified her now, ma'am. Her name's Eileen Deeley; née Eileen Phillips. She was born in Belfast, although her parents moved to Liverpool in 1995. We're looking into her birth father. Alan Phillips. Gerry Deeley's her stepfather.

'The family did a moonlight flit so we suspect Alan Phillips must either have been involved in something or come to the attention of someone and been threatened.

That could have some significance for the kidnapping of her daughter, I suppose, but it was a long time ago.'

'There might be a background of criminality in the family then, Chief Inspector. Mr Pedersen might have been correct about the girl's friends. She might have been mixing with the criminal underworld in Oslo,' Wilkinson suggested.

'Maybe.' Gawn shrugged.

'Or she could have been in touch with criminal elements here, couldn't she?' Wilkinson added. 'Maybe some old friends of her father's?' She sat back in her chair, taking her glasses off her nose and twirling them thoughtfully by one leg.

'She was only about three when she left Belfast,' Gawn said, 'and, according to her mother, they haven't set eyes on her father since the day he walked out on them in Liverpool.'

Gawn knew she was deliberately keeping Wilkinson in the dark. Marie Deeley hadn't seen her husband but Nina had seen her father. She would tell the ACC, but not just yet. Not until she was sure what it meant.

'You know this craze for tracing your family and your ancestors, Chief Inspector,' McWilliams said, turning in her chair to look at Gawn. Gawn had almost forgotten the woman was there. 'Your victim might have fancied going back to some of her father's old haunts and asking questions about him.'

'And asked the wrong person.' Wilkinson finished the sentence for her.

'It's possible,' Gawn conceded. 'We can check into that when we know more about Alan Phillips and what he might have got himself into. But the photograph, ma'am,' Gawn began, bringing them back to the point of the meeting.

'We've never done anything like this before. I've checked,' McWilliams said. 'Obviously we release pictures of missing people and victims after someone has been arrested and charged but we don't even release mug shots of convicted villains like some other forces do. Well, not usually and never something… like this.'

Gawn realised McWilliams must have been shown the picture. It was just as well she hadn't seen the video as well, she thought.

'What are your thoughts on this, Chief Inspector? What would your recommendation be?' Wilkinson asked.

Oh, oh. There it was. She was being invited to step into this pile of crap; take responsibility for the decision. If there was a backlash, it would have been her decision. Ass-covering again.

If she said, 'do it', there'd be outrage. Groups would protest the invasion of the rights of the victim; others would be horrified that the police were stooping to new tactics to frighten the public. There would be fear that a violent gang was on the loose and suddenly the story would be front page news. And there would be all kinds of conspiracy theories.

If she said, 'don't do it', she really didn't think it would end well for Nina. The kidnappers would react badly and she would pay the penalty.

'I don't think we have very much choice, ma'am,' said Gawn eventually. 'The kidnappers were very clear on what they wanted and I don't doubt for a minute there would be serious repercussions for the victims if we don't comply.'

Wilkinson was nodding, her spectacles back on the end of her nose making her look like a wise little owl from a children's story book. She'd need the wisdom of Solomon for this one, Gawn thought.

'Can we clean the image up a bit? Maybe use some filters to soften it,' Wilkinson suggested to McWilliams.

'We can try,' McWilliams said, 'but it'll still look like someone who's been beaten and is terrified.'

'That's exactly what the kidnappers want,' Gawn said.

She'd had one of her 'lightbulb moments' as one of her previous bosses at the Met had called them.

'They must be hoping we make an announcement. Maybe they want to get a message out there – not to Pedersen – he already knows Nina and Norrie have been kidnapped. I think the kidnappers want someone else to know, someone they can't contact directly for whatever reason.'

Gawn thought she knew now who that was.

Wilkinson was nodding thoughtfully. 'You could be right, Chief Inspector,' she said.

'And I think we should be identifying our victim by her other name when we release the photograph,' Gawn said.

'Deeley?' McWilliams asked.

'Phillips. From the beginning I wondered why they'd been grabbed here. It would have been so much easier to do it in England. But now I think it's something to do with Eileen's past. It wasn't a fluke they were kidnapped here. I think it's all to do with Belfast in 1995.'

Chapter 43

McWilliams wasted no time. First mentions of the couple on the local newspaper's website and the PSNI's Facebook account went out mid-afternoon along with a copy of the photograph. It was picked up by the radio and TV channels and Gawn saw it on the five o'clock news.

The photograph had been edited. It was impossible to make out too many details of her injuries but the name Eileen Phillips was now out in the public domain. And they had issued a picture of Norrie and of the couple's distinctive campervan.

> *Police are becoming increasingly concerned for the welfare of a pair of missing tourists. Eileen Deeley, also known as Eileen Phillips, and Norbert Pedersen were visiting Northern Ireland when they were reported missing at the weekend.*

The PSNI has now issued photographs of the missing woman and man. Chief Inspector Gawn Girvin, who is leading the investigation team, said, 'Ms Phillips is in a distressed condition in a recent photograph we have obtained and we are very keen to find her and her travelling companion.'

'Well, that should keep our kidnappers happy,' Maxwell said as he watched and listened over Gawn's shoulder.

'Hopefully,' she said. 'Now let's see where we are in the investigation. The clock's ticking, Paul. We only have two days before Pedersen needs to hand over the ransom and we've still no idea who we're dealing with, do we?'

She wasn't being critical of Maxwell. She knew he and everyone else was working flat out.

'Did Jack find anyone of interest travelling over to London on Sunday?' Gawn asked.

'No. No names nor faces popped out to him. No known villains. And, you know, they could have travelled from Dublin and they may not have flown directly to London,' he added.

'What about Maitland? Anything useful from him or the Drugs Squad?' she asked, not expecting anything. He would have told her if he'd got some good news.

'No. Maitland couldn't suggest who might be involved. And Jack's friend in the Drugs Squad says it doesn't sound like the kind of thing any of the organised drugs gangs would be getting involved with. They use violence, OK, but not something like this. This takes more organisation and patience than they have.'

'Human Trafficking?' Gawn suggested.

'No. There's always plenty on the dark web but they haven't come across any chatter about a kidnapping or anyone offering videos of Nina being tortured. They promised to keep an eye out.'

Nothing. Gawn could almost hear a clock ticking in her head.

Chapter 44

Sam Rainey laughed as she walked into the ladies toilets and found Gawn brushing her hair. 'We'll have to stop meeting like this or people will be talking about us,' she said.

'The old boys will think we're hatching some plot against them,' Gawn replied with a smile. 'Sorry I haven't had time to ask how things are going on your case,' she added. 'I meant to do it.'

'I know. You've been busy on your own. I understand.'

'Well?' Gawn said.

'You want an update now? Here?'

Rainey seemed surprised and slightly reticent to comply. Gawn guessed she might be embarrassed at a lack of progress.

'Yes. I know it's unconventional, but, hey, what the heck! You're here, I'm here and I have five minutes before I need to get back.'

Rainey pushed her fringe back out of her eyes.

'Well, the CSIs found an interesting fingerprint on one of the drawers of Fraser's filing cabinet.'

She stopped and seemed reluctant to go on.

'That's good. I'm sure Fraser didn't let just anybody touch his filing cabinet,' Gawn said, remembering what Rainey had told her about the housekeeper not even being allowed to dust it. 'Whose print is it?'

'I don't know. But we have it on record in relation to a cold case.'

'Which case?' Gawn asked with only a casual interest, her mind half on the kidnapping and her own victims again.

'A car bombing in 1995. Two of our own were killed.'

Rainey didn't need to go on. Gawn knew which case it was. She found herself reaching out and clutching the side of the hand basin for support as her head began to swim and the room began to revolve around her. The last thing she heard far in the distance was Rainey's anxious voice.

'Are you alright, Gawn?'

Rainey reached out and grabbed the DCI's arm to stop her from falling.

It was the murder of her father and his partner.

Chapter 45

Rainey guided a visibly wobbly detective chief inspector to her own office and fetched a glass of water. Fortunately, they met no one on the way.

Gawn waited until her heart had stopped thumping in her chest and her hands had stopped shaking before dismissing Rainey. She didn't explain why she had reacted as she had, just made the DI promise that she would tell no one what had happened. Next, she phoned Maxwell and asked him to come to her office.

'You fainted? In the ladies toilets? You're not pregnant, are you, boss?' Maxwell asked suspiciously.

'No. Of course, I'm not,' she said. 'Sam told me that the CSIs had found a fingerprint connected to my father's murder at Fraser's crime scene.'

'Your father's murder?' Maxwell repeated slowly.

His face was a mixture of shock and concern. She was aware she must look pale and cursed to herself that she never carried make-up to work. At least then she could have introduced a bit of colour to her cheeks to hide her reaction to Rainey's news.

'Is she saying someone who was involved in your father's murder might be Fraser's killer too?'

His voice was half an octave higher than usual. 'It was nearly thirty years ago,' he added in a small voice.

'She's not saying that, Paul. All the fingerprint proves is that someone who handled the bomb that killed him was also inside Fraser's home sometime probably over the weekend around the time of his murder.'

'Bloody hell!'

Maxwell flopped down into the chair opposite her.

'Fraser had lots of dubious clients. You know that, Paul. It's how he made his big money. But when he started out, back in the day, he was a trainee in the firm that defended the three men who were convicted for their part in the bombing. They weren't the bombmakers, just minor characters. Gophers. Hoods. They'd have been out of prison long ago but we have their prints on file. Sam's already checked. It wasn't one of them.'

Gawn had never talked about her father or his murder. Maxwell knew he had been blown up in a car bombing but he didn't know any of the details.

'Who did they get for it in the end?' he asked.

'Just the three accessories who provided some of the components and transported it to the scene. Nobodies. Charlie Saxsby and Madas Tate, and his younger brother, Niall.'

'Madas? What sort of name is that?' Maxwell asked.

'James Tate. You must have heard of the Tates, Paul. Everyone knew James as "Madas" from "as mad as a hatter", you know? He was crazy. Total headache. His da, Norman Tate, ran a nasty wee fiefdom – protection money, extortion. Every scam under the sun. You name it, Tate's gang had a finger in it. I suppose they were the original OCG here.

'Madas was the prince in waiting to his father's empire. But he was impatient to take over and he was working very hard to prove himself as a hard man. He wasn't political.

He'd do anyone's dirty work for them if the price was right. He didn't care who his victims were, you see. If you got in his way, or someone paid him enough, he'd off you.

'They suspected he'd killed at least six people the year before my father. He was a gun for hire to the highest bidder.'

'Or a bomber,' Maxwell added. 'Do you think it would be worth our while having a chat with Madas or these other two?'

'I'm not sure they're even still alive, Paul, and there's no clear connection between them and our case. And we've plenty to be doing without chasing after coincidences. We don't have time to waste. Sam will be bringing them in for a chat, I'm sure, if they're still around.'

Gawn had sounded positive but Maxwell knew she didn't believe in coincidences. If he could have read her mind, he would have known she was beginning to put together her own theories about how the two cases were linked and where she fitted into everything.

Chapter 46

The knocking on her office door was loud and urgent, interrupting their conversation.

'Come,' Gawn called and looked across at Maxwell, her left eyebrow raised in the familiar questioning gesture he knew well.

She was feeling better. She hoped she looked normal again. She didn't want any office gossip about her being pregnant and she didn't want anything to distract them from finding their two victims. She hoped this was some good news. She needed that. They all did.

Jack Dee almost fell into the room in his rush. The normally phlegmatic officer was more excited than she had ever seen him.

'They've found the campervan, ma'am.'

'Where?' Maxwell asked before Gawn had time to react.

'In a reservoir outside Carrickfergus.'

Gawn knew exactly where he meant. She had driven past it only the previous week with Seb when she had accompanied him on a shopping trip to his favourite butcher in Ballynure. That all seemed like a lifetime ago now.

'A couple of fishermen spotted it. Apparently, the water level fluctuates and it's a bit lower than usual today. It would have been higher at the weekend.'

'Any bodies?' Gawn asked.

She didn't expect them to have found any bodies. At least she hoped not. Not Nina's anyway. The girl had been alive at least for a while for the photographs and video to be taken. She wasn't so sure about Norrie.

'No bodies inside the van that they could see and none found so far in the water but it's a big reservoir. It'll take some searching. They say a couple of days probably,' Dee said.

Maxwell stood up. 'I'll go out and supervise the recovery of the van,' he said.

'We need that van out quickly, Paul. I know they'll want to take their time and ensure they don't lose any forensics but we don't have any time to waste. Make sure whoever the CSM is knows that. If needs be, I'll speak to them myself.'

'I can manage, boss.'

Gawn was sure he could, but she was itching to see the van and learn what it could tell them.

'I'll go with you.'

* * *

The journey to Carrickfergus, on the road that was so familiar to her, had passed in almost total silence. Gawn was never one for casual chatter when she was driving. Maxwell was used to it, although it had unsettled him when he had first started working with her.

He had a lot on his mind too. He was still mulling over the news about Gawn's father. She had never spoken of him at all or what had happened to him, but of course, Maxwell had known. Everyone had. It had been the talk of the place before she arrived from England to take up her position as DCI. She had been a child at the time of the murder. It probably explained her reserve and the protective shell she had built around herself. Until she met Sebastian York, she had let no one get close to her. Her nickname had been the Ice Queen.

Gawn had been thinking about her father too. She knew he would have expected her to find the kidnapped man and woman no matter how hard she had to work and he wouldn't have let anything going on in his personal life interfere with that. She put thoughts of him and what had happened to him out of her mind.

She had also been thinking about her involvement in the case. She couldn't believe that the chief constable had chanced upon her among all the senior officers available to him to lead this inquiry. She had never really believed that. It was down to Sir Patrick Montgomery – whoever he really was. Somewhere in all this she sensed his guiding hand. And the coincidence of Denton Fraser being killed the same weekend as the kidnapping was ringing loud alarm bells for her. There had to be a connection and the unidentified fingerprint proved that for her.

They passed the PSNI's facility at Seapark where the van would eventually be taken for forensic examination. Then she left the wide highway to drive up Trooperslane and over the railway line, the same line which, further along, ran in front of her house. Of course, they were held up at the level crossing waiting for a train to pass. It was not a busy line, with trains running only as far as Larne Harbour. Just her luck then to arrive at the same time as one of the infrequent trains. Gawn tapped her fingers on the steering wheel and bit her lip in frustration while she waited.

Once the barrier lifted, she took off, squealing the tyres in her haste. New Line was closed off with crime scene tape. A police car was blocking it and a policeman was busy explaining to annoyed-looking drivers that they needed to detour. Yellow diversion signs were already in place by the side of the road and traffic was building up. The local officer recognised Gawn's car so they were waved through, garnering glares from waiting motorists.

Both detectives knew they would lose what was left of the light very soon.

When they rounded a bend in the twisty little mountain road, Gawn and Maxwell could see arc lights had already been put in place. The steep bank of the reservoir was illuminated to help the searchers.

Gawn drew her car to the side of the road, leaving Maxwell enough room to get out without having to step into the sheugh. The two were handed shoe covers and gloves by a fresh-faced constable who looked excited to be part of the investigation. Gawn thought he looked very young or maybe it was just that she was beginning to feel her age. This might be his first serious crime scene. He would never forget it. She could still remember hers.

They signed the crime scene log. Gawn leaned on Maxwell's shoulder as she pulled the forensic coverings over her trainers.

As Maxwell balanced precariously on one leg to put on his own covers, she said, 'Lean on me, for goodness' sake, Paul. We don't want you keeling over. It isn't a good look for a DI. They'd be gossiping that you'd been drinking on duty.' She smiled but she was only half-joking. She always worried that was the way rumours started.

They walked past a row of parked cars, mainly police vehicles, and a little group, made up mostly of CSIs and police officers, watching the work going on to retrieve the campervan. There were two men in Barbour jackets and welly boots clutching fishing rods in the group as well.

A slightly battered-looking recovery truck was slowly winching the gaily coloured campervan out of the reservoir. Inch by screeching inch, it emerged out of the water, the noise of the winch grating on Gawn's ears. It sounded like some prehistoric monster in pain rising from the depths in a horror movie.

The van, dangling from the tow truck's chain at a precarious angle, looked pathetic. It was like some child's discarded toy with silly cartoon figures emblazoned in bright primary colours over the sides. Water gushed out from underneath in mini waterfalls. The doors were still closed and the windows were intact. Perhaps they would be in luck and there would still be some useful evidence to be found inside.

Two shiny black heads, like a pair of playful seals, suddenly bobbed up out of the water near the bank. The divers emerged and were helped up the steep side by uniformed officers. They padded towards Gawn and Maxwell, their flippers making them look ungainly. They would have passed by without a word but Gawn held up her hand and stopped them.

'Find anything down there?'

One of the men squinted to make out the name on her lanyard before answering.

'It's a bit too dark to see much, ma'am. But there's nothing obvious near the van. We'll need to start again in the morning. And maybe bring in another couple of divers too, if we can. It's a big area to search.'

'And there's weeds and stuff over the other side where a body could get tangled up,' the other diver added.

'But there's no current in the reservoir, is there?' Gawn asked. 'You wouldn't expect a body to move too far from where it went into the water.'

'Probably not, ma'am,' the first diver said. 'If it was weighted down, it wouldn't budge much at all.'

She nodded to dismiss them and they walked off towards their own van pulling their hoods off over their heads as they moved away.

'Welcome back, Chief Inspector.'

Gawn spun round at the friendly greeting. It was Mark Ferguson. He had been crime scene manager on several of her cases in the past. She knew he could be quick so she was glad to see him. They had less than forty-eight hours until the ransom was to be paid and they still had no idea who was holding their two victims, or where.

'You know what I'm going to say, don't you, Mark?' Gawn asked looking around at the churned-up ground and noticed tyre tracks. If anyone could find her something useful here, it would be Ferguson.

'I can guess. You want whatever we find asap. Like, yesterday,' he joked.

She nodded. 'Yes. Please.'

'We'll do what we can. I'll be supervising here. The van will be going to the lab. At least that's not too far away. They should be able to get to work on it quickly.'

'Tonight,' Gawn insisted. 'I can't wait until tomorrow. And if they find anything, I want to know about it. Right away.'

Chapter 47

'Do you want to have a word with them yourself, boss?' Maxwell asked.

Gawn had been standing looking around. She liked to get a sense of a crime scene and was wondering why this spot had been chosen to dispose of the van. Was it just a matter of expediency? The kidnappers had moved the van from the car park in the town centre. The car park was less than two miles away. Driving around on the open road meant having to risk security cameras or passing police cars.

If they had set the van on fire, the smoke would have been noticed quickly. Had they simply used the nearest place they could find to dispose of it? Or had they known about the reservoir and planned to dump it here but not realised the water level would change and reveal the van? That probably meant they were not local. Also, did it mean Nina and Norrie might be somewhere nearby?

She had plenty of questions. And no answers.

Maxwell had been off talking to the local sergeant and then questioning the two men who had discovered the van in the water and phoned the police. He had just walked back to her side.

'Yes. I'll have a quick word,' she said.

'This is Norman Nabney and this is Keith Nelson,' Maxwell said and nodded at each man in turn. 'Detective Chief Inspector Girvin.'

The men were looking a little bewildered.

'We just came out for a couple of hours of fishing. We didn't think we were going to end up in the middle of all this,' Nabney said and looked around him bemused.

He was the older of the two. He was dressed in a pair of well-worn brown corduroy trousers, baggy at the knees, and a Barbour jacket. His welly boots were splattered with mud as if he had been clambering through hedges and over fields. The duncher he had been wearing had been removed in a gesture of respect when he was first introduced to Gawn so his head of thinning white hair added to the impression of age and respectability.

'I think I've seen you before.' He spoke slightly hesitantly, his brow wrinkled as he struggled to try to remember where. 'Do you live around here somewhere?' he asked.

'You've seen her on the telly,' Nelson interrupted. 'Last year. That sex maniac attacking women in Belfast. Remember, Norman?' Nelson nudged his companion in the ribs. There was a smile on his face as if he was pleased with himself for remembering.

Nelson was a mountain of a man, dwarfing his friend. He was almost as wide as he was tall. He wouldn't have looked out of place on a TV strongman competition. He sported a beard, long and bushy, with touches of dirty grey in among the mousy brown. His quilted shooting vest worn over a check shirt was strained across his ample stomach. A long thin canvas bag was slung over his shoulder. Gawn had seen fishermen at the harbour in Carrick, from the balcony of her old apartment, using the same sort of bag to carry their rods. He had a net in one hand and a square bucket with a lid in the other.

'Do you fish up here often?' Gawn asked, directing her question to Nelson, hoping to distract him from making any further comments about her case from last year.

'As often as we can,' the man replied. 'When you pay for the rod licence, you want to get your money's worth, don't you?' he laughed.

His laughter made him break out into a prolonged bout of coughing and sneezing. He produced a slightly grubby-looking handkerchief and wiped his mouth gathering sputum into it before putting it back into his pocket.

Gawn waited until he had finished before she asked, 'What time did you get here this afternoon? Did you come together?'

Nabney answered for them. 'About three. I'm retired, you see. I can come anytime but I prefer to have a wee bit of company. It's nice to get a bit of chat. I live alone. But Keith's still working so we had to wait until the end of his shift.'

'Where do you work, Mr Nelson?' Gawn asked.

'I'm a delivery driver for the local supermarket. I finished my last run just after two. I went home to get changed and then called for Norman. We came up in my car.' He pointed towards a battered-looking red Ford sitting parked between two police cars.

'There was no one else here when you arrived. You didn't see anyone leaving?' Gawn asked.

She didn't think the van had only been dumped today. It would have been too risky for the kidnappers to have been driving around in daylight after all the publicity. It had probably been here at least since last night, if not longer. But how long? Had it been here since it left the car park on Friday or had it been hidden somewhere nearby?

The men shook their heads.

'When did you notice the vehicle in the water?' Gawn asked.

'Maybe about four o'clock or just after. You'll have a record of the time we called it in, won't you?' Nelson asked. 'We decided to move a bit further up away from the road before it got too dark. We weren't having much luck down here, you see. When we got up there' – he nodded towards where the van was being slowly lowered onto its four wheels – 'the water level had gone down since the weekend and we saw the roof of the van.'

'You were here at the weekend?' Maxwell asked.

'I told you. We like to get our money's worth,' Nelson said and laughed again.

'And you're sure the van wasn't here then?' Gawn asked.

'Well, we mightn't have been quite so far up on Sunday, but there were others up there. They would have seen it, I'm sure,' Nabney told them.

If someone had seen it, they hadn't reported it.

'You didn't move up here because you'd noticed the tracks leading from the car park and decided to have a look?' Gawn asked.

The men exchanged a look and Nabney shook his head.

123

'We noticed them, but we didn't think too much about the tracks, to be honest. Sometimes cars come up past the car park to get further away off the road. This is a good spot for courting couples, you see,' he explained. 'You have to be careful not to see too much, if you know what I mean,' Nabney added, and smiled.

It was a long time since Gawn had heard anyone referring to 'courting couples' and she wondered if it was only couples he was careful to turn a blind eye to. This would be a good spot for lots of other things too. Dumping vehicles among them.

Chapter 48

Gawn was lying wide awake. She'd known she wouldn't be able to sleep but Seb had insisted she needed to rest. He was snoring rhythmically beside her, his face resting on his hand like a baby. She was lying on her back trying to move as little as possible. She didn't want to wake him.

She'd spent the last hour rerunning the interview with the two fishermen in her mind. They had looked like typical fishermen or at least how she thought typical fishermen looked. They had seemed happy to answer her questions but she remembered one quick glance between them when she'd asked about the tyre tracks. Ferguson had later explained that he thought he could identify the tracks of the van but the ground was too badly churned up and muddy to get any footprints.

Still Gawn wondered if they had seen something. Or someone. It had been only a millisecond of a look on Nelson's face, a warning sideways movement of his eyes towards his friend to say nothing or perhaps an indication that he was afraid Nabney would reveal something. She'd spent too much time in interview rooms reading body language and facial expressions not to have noticed it.

But maybe it meant nothing. She might be reading too much into it. She'd get Jack Dee to talk to the locals and check Nelson's and Nabney's backgrounds. She didn't think they were the kidnappers but they might know something.

She jumped when her mobile phone vibrated loudly in the silence. She made a lunge for it, but only managed to swipe it off her bedside table.

'Damn!'

'Wh- What?' Seb muttered and his eyes flickered open for an instant.

She had almost fallen out of the bed stretching to retrieve the phone from the floor where it had fallen. She glanced back to tell Seb to go back to sleep but he was already snoring again.

'Girvin,' she hissed in a half whisper not wanting to wake him.

She expected news. She hoped for it but now she didn't know whether to be excited or dread it when it seemed she was about to get some. Maybe they had found Nina and Norrie.

'You said to let you know if we found anything.'

She recognised Ferguson's voice. He sounded tired. He must have been working at the site since she had met him there.

'What? Was it the tyre tracks?'

'No. They're just the tracks from the van, like I told you. We couldn't get tracks for any other vehicle except your two fishermen's car or any clear footprints either. The kidnappers probably had another vehicle to take them away from the reservoir but they must have parked it on the roadway. No tracks.'

'What have you found then, Mark?'

'It's what we didn't find,' he said.

'What?'

'No cameras, no laptop, no SD cards, nothing. Whoever dumped the van took all that stuff out of it first.'

'So they'd be able to keep on uploading the vlogs,' she suggested.

'Maybe. I don't know anything about that. It could be vehicle thieves, stripping the van of anything valuable.'

She didn't think so. Vlogs had been uploaded after the time they now thought the couple had been abducted. Someone, either Norrie or the kidnappers, had been misdirecting them.

'Did you find anything at all to help?' she asked.

'A cigarette butt inside the van.'

'A cigarette butt?'

She was disappointed. She didn't know exactly what she had hoped for but a cigarette butt didn't sound as if it could be very helpful after being submerged in water.

'They might be able to get some DNA from it. There's a new technique they're gonna try. Do either of your victims smoke?' Ferguson asked.

'I don't know,' she admitted. 'But I'll find out. If it's not theirs, then it would place someone else in the van for us.'

'Aye. They'll start work on it in the morning. They might have a result for you some time tomorrow, if you're very lucky.'

'Fast track it, Mark. We need to know who was in the van.'

She knew that just because the cigarette was inside the van it didn't mean it belonged to one of the kidnappers. It could be theirs or belong to someone they had met on their journey and invited into their van. Like her father, or someone perfectly innocent. Anyway, the most likely explanation was it belonged to one of the victims.

'And thanks, Mark.'

'Hey, that's not the best bit,' Ferguson said as she sounded as if she was going to end the call. 'We found a phone as well.'

She realised he had been keeping the best for last.

'It's a bit bashed about but you might be able to retrieve some information from it.'

Gawn sat up in bed. She was wide awake now.

'Get it to–'

'It's already on its way.'

'Thanks, Mark.'

This time she did end the call.

Who did the phone belong to? Nina or Norrie? Maybe they'd received threatening messages or arranged to meet someone in the forest. There could be text messages which could help them trace who the couple had been in contact with or what they had been up to.

Of course, it could also belong to one of the kidnappers dropped in a struggle. That would be the ultimate find if someone with a criminal record had dropped their phone inside the van.

She couldn't allow herself to even hope that.

Chapter 49

Thursday

The pain was bad. Getting worse. It felt as if the knife was stabbing into her over and over again; as if Sneezy, the man with evil eyes, was back and wanted to finish the job this time. She knew he wanted to kill her, was just awaiting his chance.

His eyes were the only parts of him she had seen. They were cold and dead. Only when he had leaned over her body to check her wound had she seen something different. It was pleasure and excitement. He enjoyed inflicting pain.

Sneezy had dressed her wound but there had been no words of comfort or reassurance as he moved her roughly around. Afterwards she had been left on the bare floor, uncovered. She tried not to feel sorry for herself. She told herself it would be alright again whenever she saw Norrie, whenever the ransom was paid. They would be together again and they would be free. She was trying to believe that.

But the men never talked about Norrie. Once or twice she had tried to question them but had cowered away from Sneezy's stare and threatening hand.

'Shut up, princess,' Sneezy had said as his hand grabbed her throat and squeezed until she struggled to breathe.

'Take it easy. The boss wants her in one piece,' Doc had said, putting his hand on Sneezy's arm to pull it away.

'For now,' Sneezy said and laughed.

They told her nothing. Perhaps Norrie had escaped and that was why they said nothing. Perhaps he and the police were looking for her. That was her hope. She tried to shout his name but no words came out of her mouth.

She was alone.

Chapter 50

The building was shrouded in darkness when Gawn arrived. The constable on duty in the security sanger at the gate had seemed surprised to see her. The car park was nearly empty. Overtime had been cut. There was only a skeleton night staff. The roads and streets had been almost deserted on her journey to Belfast. Even workers on early shifts hadn't set out yet. They would be stealing another five minutes in their warm beds before facing the day.

The corridors were eerily quiet too. Gawn had heard chat about budget deficits. It seemed as if she was the only person here. Once she had heard Ferguson's news, she couldn't lie in bed for another minute. This could be the breakthrough she had been waiting for. It had to be. They didn't have anything else. The ticking clock in her brain seemed louder in the deserted corridor.

Gawn was surprised to see a faint light under the door of Incident Room B. Sam Rainey's team was based there. Maybe they'd had a breakthrough too.

Gawn walked in without knocking. She was faced with an empty room. At least, at first she thought it was empty. Empty desks and the blank screens of closed-down computers were all she saw. Then, a slight movement in the corner of the room drew her attention and she saw Sam Rainey slumped over her desk.

'Are you alright?' Gawn called, walking quickly over to her.

Rainey looked up at the sound of Gawn's voice and then jerked up in her chair, her eyes wide in embarrassment.

'God, I must have fallen asleep.'

'Are you sure you're OK?'

'Yes. Yes. I'm fine.'

'What are you even doing here at this time?' Gawn asked.

'I could ask you the same thing,' Rainey replied, looking at her watch. 'I'm waiting to hear back about Fraser's phone.'

'I thought there wasn't anything useful on Fraser's phone. It was a bust for any evidence,' Gawn said.

'There wasn't anything,' Rainey told her. 'Not on his official phone, the one with a contract paid for by his business account. We'd already contacted his service provider and got everything we could from it. But then we found out he kept another phone. A burner. Surprise,

surprise,' she added sarcastically. 'His housekeeper let slip about it to me when I spoke to her again.

'They'd already searched the house from top to bottom but they hadn't found another phone. I think the killer must have taken it away with him which means there could be something incriminating on it.

'The housekeeper remembered Fraser had let her use that phone once. She'd needed to contact her daughter about something. She was out somewhere with Fraser and she'd forgotten her own phone.

'Her daughter lives in Newry so I drove there and got her phone from her. I didn't want to have to wait until her service provider gave us her call records and text messages. This was a lot quicker. I hope. I have someone trawling through her call log trying to identify his number from the approximate date and time Mrs Ritchie thinks she used Fraser's phone.

'Once they've identified it, they're going to try to ping it and see if it's turned on and where it is. I'm waiting to hear if they have any joy. I know it's a long shot, but you can't help but hope, can you?' Rainey smiled ruefully up at Gawn.

'You do know you could have waited until this morning and got some of the local guys to deliver it to Belfast for you, don't you? Or even sent one of your team to get it?' Gawn asked.

'You mean like you would have done? I was just taking a page from the Gawn Girvin playbook,' Rainey responded, tipping her head to one side and waiting for an answer.

'Fair point, Sam,' Gawn said. 'I would probably have done it myself too. But they haven't got back to you yet? I'm amazed they're even working on it tonight.'

'I called in a big favour. Otherwise, they wouldn't be.' Rainey smiled sheepishly. 'It's costing me a bottle of ten-year-old Bushmills,' she said.

'I hope it doesn't mean they're not working on the phone in my case.'

Gawn was only half joking. Resources were tight. Departments were understaffed. Rainey's phone evidence could be important but Fraser was already dead. Finding his killer wouldn't bring him back. Nina and Norrie were still alive. She hoped. Her case should have priority.

Chapter 51

Gawn had brewed herself some coffee and had just taken a sip of the almost scalding liquid when her phone rang.

'You're not going to believe this.'

It was Sam Rainey.

'What?'

'They got a ping off Fraser's phone.'

Gawn could hear the excitement in the woman's voice. She couldn't begrudge Rainey some progress, but she had hoped it was the lab with news of the phone found in the campervan.

'Brilliant. You got lucky. I'd have expected your shooter would have turned it off, if not dumped it at the bottom of Belfast Lough,' Gawn said. 'So where is it now?'

'In our lab,' Rainey replied.

'That was fast. How did you get hold of it so quickly?' Gawn asked.

'No. I mean, it *was* in our lab,' Rainey repeated slowly.

'Our lab? At Seapark?'

'Yes,' Rainey said and then paused as if she wanted to give Gawn time to digest what she had just told her. 'It's the phone from your case, Gawn. The one they found in that campervan.'

* * *

Gawn had opened the vertical blinds on her office window so the morning light was shining weakly in, vying with the central light fitting and her desk lamp, which were both still switched on. Rainey and Gawn were clutching sheets of paper and scanning them. They were printouts of the text messages for the last three months found on the phone from the campervan. Fraser's burner phone.

There were a lot of them. Organised Crime would have a field day. She would pass the information on when she had got what she needed.

'Does this mean your missing man is my shooter?' Rainey asked, sounding bemused at the idea.

'Norrie? I don't think so. I don't see him as an international assassin. I think it's more likely that your shooter is my kidnapper,' Gawn replied.

Gawn flicked over a page and began reading aloud.

> *Behold, your sins will find you out. Double-crossing bastard. We know what you did. You stitched us up. Remember Pip. We want to know where he is.*

'That seems to be the first threatening message that was sent to Fraser. At least in the last three months. They'll need to check out the number it was sent from but I expect it's another burner,' Rainey said. 'He didn't reply to it. He probably had plenty of discontented clients who hated his guts. He was good but he didn't get all the villains off. I'm sure there's more than one who would have liked to have given him a good going over.'

'Aye, but not killed him, Sam. Not execution style. That's extreme. Even the paramilitaries at the height of the Troubles didn't go in for assassinating lawyers. They needed them,' Gawn said. 'No, I think this person could have served time *because* of Fraser or at least thinks he has. Perhaps he thinks Fraser betrayed him in some way. And it must have been a serious crime, something he's done serious prison time for. You'll need to get people looking back through all of Fraser's cases.'

Rainey looked at Gawn with an expression that suggested she was horrified.

'Seriously? All? How far back? Some of my people are already looking at recent cases but I hadn't made it a priority. We were concentrating on chasing up his current clients and any threats made against him that his office staff knew about.

'We've identified some of the people who were annoyed with him and we were trying to establish their whereabouts at the time of the shooting. How far back do you think we need to go now?' Rainey asked.

'Your guess is as good as mine. Maybe thirty years? That's the kind of stretch that could make you very angry,' Gawn suggested tentatively.

'All his cases for the past thirty years! I don't think we have the manpower for that. Not to get it done quickly anyway.'

'Well, look at cases where his clients were convicted. That'd be a start. That should cut it down a bit for you. He was usually successful. This guy could be unhappy because he thinks Fraser stitched him up. And then look at where they'd got at least, say, ten years in prison.'

'It could still be a lot of cases,' Rainey said.

'And cross reference with those villains who have just recently been released. That should cut it down a bit more. But let's read on. Maybe we'll find more of a clue to the shooter's identity.'

There was silence while they scanned down the list of messages.

'Here. Friday. The day he was killed. "Don't think you can hide from us. We want Pip",' Rainey read.

'Pip again,' Gawn said.

'Do you think that's some sort of code for the proceeds of their crime? Fraser might have been holding it for them and now they want it back,' Rainey suggested.

'No. It sounds more like a person. I don't know any Pips. Do you?' Gawn said. She was biting her lower lip, a habit she had when thinking.

'The only person I've ever heard of called Pip was a character on *The Archers*,' Rainey said. 'My mother used to listen to it when I was living at home. Or there was a Pip in a book I had to read for A level. *Great Expectations*.'

'Dickens?'

'Yes.'

'I read that too. A long time ago. Wasn't the Pip in that book involved with an escaped convict? Or am I getting it confused with some other book?' Gawn asked.

'Magwitch,' Rainey announced.

'Magwitch. That's right.'

'Could it be someone who's escaped from prison recently and is out for revenge?' Rainey suggested.

'You can add that to your list of parameters if you like. Here, look. Fraser replied on Friday afternoon,' Gawn said, her finger tracing a line down the page until she came to the message. 'He must have realised who was texting him. "Can't help. He was ghosted."'

'Who? Pip?'

'Seems like it,' Gawn said.

'So, Pip is a person. What does "he was ghosted" mean? Is he dead?'

'I've heard the phrase before. The Americans I worked with used it sometimes,' Gawn answered.

'Like for detainees in Guantanamo Bay, you mean?' Rainey asked.

'Not really. More when referring to what happened to their operatives after covert operations.'

'So this Pip might have been involved in some criminal operation?' Rainey asked. Her eyes were wide open in surprise. Like Gawn, she had never worked in counterterrorism.

'Look at this one on Friday evening. It couldn't have been very long before he was killed. Fraser sent this message to a different number. Probably another burner. "They know. They're after me. Help.'"

'He knew he was in danger. Who was he trying to get to help him? Tracing that number is a priority. There was no reply to the message,' Rainey said, scanning down rest of the texts.

Gawn dialled the number which had sent the text and listened.

'It's dead. It's probably at the bottom of Belfast Lough,' she said.

Gawn was thinking. Joining dots. The fingerprint on the bomb which had killed her father. A secret operation. It had to be linked to her father's case. And who had disappeared in all this? Alan Phillips, Nina's father.

'I need to talk to somebody.'

Chapter 52

It should have been easy to contact Montgomery. He was with the Department for Business and Trade. She found his name on their website. She expected to be able to get him there. But, when Gawn had phoned London, she had been told he was on leave and wouldn't be back for at least a month. They had refused to give her any contact details.

What should she do next? The sensible thing would be to talk to Wilkinson, tell her what she had found out. But Wilkinson might not be keen to delve too deeply into the murky past of covert operations during the Troubles, which was well before her time with the PSNI. There could still be people now in positions of power who had been involved thirty years ago and wouldn't be happy to see their dirty secrets resurface.

Maybe she could phone Lynch. He might have a way of contacting Montgomery in London, if he was prepared to help her. But she didn't think he would be sticking his neck out for her or risking his career.

She dialled a number on her mobile phone. It started ringing. Within three rings it had been answered.

'Gawn?'

The voice sounded surprised but pleased.

'I didn't expect to hear from you. Not after our last tango.'

'Hello, Mike,' Gawn said.

She was phoning her ex-colleague and former lover, Mike Lee, who now ran his own security business in London. Their paths had crossed on a case in Belfast when she had had to arrest him.

'I want to use your services.'

'And what sort of services would those be, darling?' he asked suggestively.

'Your business expertise.'

'And there was me getting excited that it was my other expertise you were after,' he said and laughed.

'Fuck off, Mike.'

She surprised herself with the vehemence of her response. She was upset and worried. There were things going on outside her control and now it seemed to be getting very personal. It was as if she was caught up in a spider's web.

'I'd rather fu–'

'Do you want the job or not?' she said before he could finish.

'Depends what it is. Nothing's ever straightforward with you, darling.'

'I want everything you can get on a man called Sir Patrick Montgomery. Ostensibly he works for the Department for Business and Trade.'

'Ostensibly?'

'I can't get hold of him there. He's listed on their website but they say he's on leave. I want to know exactly who he is and where he is so I can contact him. Will you find him for me?'

'How can I refuse, darling?'

'And stop calling me darling.'

Chapter 53

Gawn was waiting to hear back from Mike. Waiting was something she didn't do well. He knew that of old, from nights spent together in draughty cars on stakeouts. She had impressed on him the urgency of getting the information and he had promised to put his best people on it. She knew that meant he would do it himself. He was just like her. He thought no one could do anything as well as he could.

Maxwell was out with some of the team overseeing a search of the area around the reservoir. It was farmland with isolated farmhouses or forestry land where it might be possible for someone to hide. It wasn't a typical door-to-door search and it would take a lot of time. He thought Nina and Norrie might be somewhere in the area. Gawn wasn't so sure.

When her phone rang, she knew it wasn't Mike. It was too soon. Even he wasn't that good.

'Girvin.'

'Gawn.'

For a second she didn't recognise the voice. Then she realised it was Aoife McWilliams.

'Yes?'

Gawn knew she sounded brusque. She didn't have time for all this PR rubbish. What did the woman want with her now? Couldn't they just let her get on with her job?

'We've had a request from *Crime Round-Up*. They want you on the show.'

Gawn knew the TV programme McWilliams had named. Like a lot of police officers, she watched it sometimes. It was interesting to see colleagues on it and they could engage in a bit of slagging afterwards about how they'd looked and sounded.

Gawn had never been on it but not because she was afraid of the slagging. There'd been requests on some of her high-profile cases but she had always managed to convince Wilkinson that someone else would do a better job of talking on camera. She was already thinking Maxwell could do it this time if they really wanted someone.

'When?' she asked.

'Tonight.'

'Tonight!'

'I know it's short notice but it's a good thing. It's only on once a month so by the time the next one comes around in four weeks your case will be…'

Gawn wondered what the woman was going to say. Solved? Cold? A murder case?

'Old news,' McWilliams said. 'They've made a space in their running order to fit you in tonight.'

Gawn wondered if they had made the space or if they had been encouraged to make a space. That was the kind of pressure Montgomery could apply, she thought. But she didn't know why he would do that.

'When would we need someone there?' Gawn asked, · thinking of how she could get Maxwell to rearrange his evening.

'You would need to be there about five o'clock. They take you through the running order for the programme, where your segment would slot in and so on. I imagine it would be somewhere near the beginning to leave time for people to phone in and then for an update before the end of the show if there'd been any helpful calls. Then, after they explain all that, it would be make-up and it all goes live at nine.'

McWilliams sounded upbeat. This was her world. She was used to it.

Gawn didn't like the way she had said *you*. She did think the programme could be useful. She knew it had high viewing figures. They could reach a lot of people and maybe someone who had missed their previous appeals might ring in with information. But the idea of taking part filled her with dread.

'I can spare Maxwell to go.'

Gawn thought he would be quite pleased to be asked to take part and his wife would be delighted about it.

'He's very photogenic,' she added. 'He'll come across well and he'll be able to give them any information that I could.'

'They asked for you, Chief Inspector. They know you're in charge of the case. Why would the SIO not want to take part? That's what they'd ask. And I must say, it's what I'd ask too. You want to find your two victims, don't you? This programme could be a real help.'

Chapter 54

'You're going to be on TV? Really?' Seb sounded surprised. And delighted. She had known he would be. He was proud of her.

Gawn had sat for five minutes after her phone conversation with McWilliams, debating with herself. She was going to have to do the interview. She couldn't see a way out of it. She decided she'd better let Seb know if only because it meant she would be late home and that would worry him, and he would be disappointed if she appeared on television without telling him. She knew he'd be on the phone with his mother and his two sisters alerting them as soon as they'd finished speaking.

'What time?' he asked.

'The programme's on at nine. I think my starring role should be near the beginning, or so I've been told.'

'Don't forget to tell them to use your good side.'

Seb was teasing her.

'I'd prefer it if they were using Maxwell's good side, Seb. You know I hate this kind of thing.'

'But if it helps find your kidnapped couple, surely it's worthwhile.'

'Yes. You're right. Anyway, I must get back to work. I just wanted to let you know.'

'Thank you, babe. You'll smash it. Break a leg.'

'I'm not acting in a play, Seb,' she began but the line was dead. He had already rung off.

As soon as she replaced the receiver, there was a knock on her door. It was Maxwell.

'Find anything?' she asked.

'Give us a chance. It's a lot of ground to cover. But I do have some news. They got a match for the DNA from the cigarette.'

'Really?' Gawn said, all thoughts of TV interviews forgotten.

'I think they even surprised themselves at being able to do it. It was a long shot. Some new technique they were trying. It depended on how long the cigarette had been submerged. They hoped they'd be able to get something but they didn't know if it would give them enough for an ID. It did and they matched it straight off.'

Maxwell was pleased. He was practically grinning from ear to ear. Gawn smiled back at him.

'Who is it?' she asked.

'Joey Mancarelli.'

Her brow furrowed. 'The name doesn't mean anything to me, Paul.'

'He's a small-time hood. But he's on the fringes of the Tate gang.'

The Tates again.

'But,' continued Maxwell, 'the interesting thing is, Mancarelli likes knives. They're his speciality.'

Their eyes locked as they thought of the video they had watched together.

'He has convictions for ABH using a knife. It's his weapon of choice.'

'We need to find him, Paul. He has some explaining to do about how his DNA got inside that van.'

'We're already all over it.'

Chapter 55

Gawn was sitting behind her desk, every few seconds glancing at the mobile phone beside her. She was willing it to ring. Mike hadn't phoned back yet and it was almost three o'clock. Only two hours until she'd have to present herself at the TV studios. She felt like a sacrificial lamb. She'd be unreachable until after the show had finished. She couldn't bear the thought of being out of the loop and not knowing what was going on, having to leave it all to Maxwell. He would do a good job. He was perfectly capable of questioning Mancarelli if they could find him, but she wanted to be there.

Her phone rang. It was Maxwell.

'They've got Mancarelli. They picked him up in a bar in the city centre. Jamie and Jack are bringing him in now. Want to join me in the interview room?'

'Better take Sam with you. I'll watch.'

* * *

'Mr Mancarelli, have you been told why you've been brought in?' Maxwell asked.

Maxwell and Rainey were sitting side by side, facing a man whose flattened nose and vicious-looking scar under his eye suggested a past involving violence. Gawn knew from his records that Mancarelli had once been a serious prospect for a major boxing title, fighting regularly on bills at the Ulster and King's Halls before his first conviction and prison stretch. After that, he had employed his talents differently, as a fixer and enforcer, a heavy for various criminal gangs but especially for the Tates.

'I heard your two goons saying something about Denton Fraser,' he answered and an ugly sneer crossed his face.

'You knew Mr Fraser?' Rainey asked.

He smirked. 'Everybody knew Mr Fraser.'

'Did you ever employ his services?'

'He was a wee bit too pricey for me, love,' he said.

Gawn squirmed as she watched. She hated being referred to as 'love' by any toerag she was questioning. She was sure Rainey did too but the DI didn't rise to his bait. She ignored the comment and went on with her questions.

'You never met him then?'

Mancarelli shook his head and tried to look sad at disappointing her. But it didn't work.

'Or been in contact with him?' Rainey pressed.

He shook his head again and then yawned long and loudly.

'Is this gonna take much longer, love? I'm a busy man. Things to do, you know.'

'It's not "love", Mr Mancarelli. I'm Detective Inspector Rainey,' she said.

Mancarelli tried to stare her out but she wouldn't look away and eventually he did.

'Where were you on Friday night?' she asked.

'Last Friday night?'

'Yes. Last Friday night,' she repeated.

'I was at home with my girlfriend.'

'All night?' Rainey asked.

'Yes. All night. She cooked me a nice wee dinner and we watched some stupid shite on TV, one of those reality things that she likes and then we went to bed.'

'And your girlfriend will confirm that, will she?'

'Of course.'

Mancarelli seemed confident. His answers had come easily. He replied almost as if he was surprised that they were doubting his word. He tried to look disappointed.

'We'll need her details. Name. Address. Phone number so we can contact her,' Rainey added.

'Do you want her measurements too? She's a 36, 24, 36.' Mancarelli laughed.

Rainey ignored him and slid a page and a pen across the table. He took his mobile out of his pocket and checked a number.

'I can never remember her phone number. She's one of many. I'm a popular boy. Much in demand. Would you like my measurements too?' He laughed again.

Rainey and Maxwell exchanged a look. He had a mobile phone but he could have bought a new one to replace one he had lost. It proved nothing.

'That me then?' Mancarelli said, snapping the pen down on the table and standing up.

'Not quite, Mr Mancarelli,' Maxwell said pleasantly. 'Sit down, please.'

Slowly, the heavy sat down again pulling the chair out further from the table and sitting back, making himself more comfortable. Maxwell shuffled a sheaf of papers in his hand. Gawn knew there was nothing pertinent to the interview on the pages. It was a tactic to get Mancarelli nervous, wondering what they had on him.

'When did you meet Nina and Norrie?'

'Who?'

The thug was making a good attempt at feigning complete bewilderment.

'Norbert Pedersen and Nina… or should I say, Eileen Phillips? They travelled here from Norway.'

Gawn had been watching Mancarelli's face. His eyes had dilated at the mention of Eileen's name. He had heard of her. He knew her. By that name.

'I've never been to Norway, Inspector. I haven't even got a passport. Never been out of good ol' Norn Ireland,' he said, but he wasn't sounding so comfortable now.

'They've been travelling around in a campervan. I'm surprised you haven't seen the appeals we've put out for help finding them,' Maxwell explained.

'I never read anything the PSNI puts out, Inspector. Load of shite, the lot of it,' Mancarelli said.

He didn't quite spit on the floor, but he looked as if he would have liked to. Maxwell ignored both the words and the look.

'You met them somewhere, Joey. You were in their van,' Maxwell said slowly with a confidence which seemed to shake the thug.

Gawn was watching closely on the monitor. She knew the two detectives would be watching his reactions too. This time, there was a fraction of a second of hesitation before Mancarelli responded. Maybe even a flicker of fear in his eyes.

'Not me, Inspector. You've got the wrong man. When was I supposed to be in this van?'

That was a key question. One Maxwell couldn't answer yet. They couldn't be sure exactly when Mancarelli had been in the van. Sometime before the two had been kidnapped? While they were being kidnapped? When the van was being abandoned in the reservoir? It could be any of those times.

'We have your DNA inside the van,' Maxwell said.

'Must be some mistake, like I said. My DNA? Inside their sodding van?'

Mancarelli was playing the innocent.

'Yes. Your DNA. We can place you in the van of the missing couple who we suspect have been killed, so you could be facing a murder charge, Joey.'

'I thought they were just kidnapped,' Mancarelli said and then put his hand up to his mouth.

'How did you know about that, Joey?'

'Word on the street. Everybody knows it. Don't think your wee press release about them going missing is fooling anybody. Not when your boss lady is in charge of the case. I've heard she's like one of those supermodel bitches. She doesn't get out of bed for anything less than a murder.' He laughed, regaining a little of his confidence and swagger.

Gawn watched as Mancarelli's eyes flicked around the room. Maxwell was holding back on questions. He knew the man was considering what he should tell them. What story would he come up with next?

'Look, I did meet them. OK? Once. Just one time.'

Gawn let out her breath out slowly. She hadn't even realised she was holding it.

'Where?' Maxwell asked after a pause, letting Mancarelli stew wondering what he would ask next.

'Portrush.'

'When?'

'On Wednesday.'

'Why were you meeting them?' Maxwell asked.

'They were in a wee spot of bother, Inspector. They'd crossed some people it's better not crossing.'

Maxwell frowned.

'They owed money for drugs and they hadn't paid,' Mancarelli explained.

Gawn pursed her lips together. Drugs. Drugs had been mentioned before. Was this all to do with drugs? Had they fallen foul of some drug dealer? Were they being taught a lesson?

'And you were sent in as a frightener?' Maxwell suggested.

'I was sent in to give them a friendly warning that they needed to pay up or else.'

'Or else what, Joey?' Maxwell asked.

'That wasn't down to me, Inspector. I was only the messenger. They didn't owe me any money. I was just paid a ton to show them the error of their ways. I sat down with them nice and reasonable, had a wee cup of some horrible herbal tea the girl made.' He turned up his nose at the thought. 'And smoked a friendly cigarette which annoyed them. They wanted me to stand outside in the rain to smoke. As if! Then I left. They were in one piece when I left.' Mancarelli sat back in his chair and folded his arms across his chest.

Gawn had flinched at his use of the expression "one piece". Was that a reference to the threat to send them back in pieces?

She felt a flutter of disappointment. Maxwell had been careful not to mention anything to do with a cigarette. She wasn't sure where that left them. They could place him inside the van but not prove that he had done anything to Nina and Norrie.

'That was in the car park in Portrush up near the amusements, you know? They were fine when I left them,' Mancarelli added. 'I'm sure you'll be able to get them on some of your spy cameras somewhere after that to prove that I didn't do anything to them.'

Of course, they could. Nina and Norrie had filmed at Dunluce Castle after that and their van had made it to Carrickfergus.

'They told me they were going to pay up. They could get the money, they said. That's all I know. Your press release said they were seen after that on their way down the coast, didn't it?'

'I thought you said you never read anything the PSNI puts out?' Maxwell said.

Mancarelli snorted.

'Who were you working for, Joey? Who did they owe money to?'

'No comment. You've got everything from me you're going to get. I think I need a lawyer now. Not Fraser, unfortunately,' he said, and laughed.

Chapter 56

Gawn met Maxwell and Rainey in the corridor outside the interview suite after Mancarelli had been taken to a cell to await the arrival of his solicitor.

'I notice you didn't press Joey about being in Fraser's house,' Gawn commented.

'No, I didn't,' said Rainey. 'It's not his phone you found. It's Fraser's. He might be the person who dropped it in the campervan, which would link him to Fraser and maybe the murder, but we can't prove that.

'The fingerprint on the filing cabinet wasn't his either, remember? And the CCTV is inconclusive at best. It could be him or hundreds of other men. It would never stand up in court. We never get a good look at the shooter's face. And Mancarelli is known for using a knife not a gun.'

'So, what's your next move then?' Gawn asked.

'Check his alibi. Talk to his girlfriend. See if we can shake her and keep checking the CCTV. And I'll get a search warrant for his house and all his electronics. He might have something on a computer that will link him to Fraser.'

'Keep at it, Sam. He's involved in something. I grant you he might not be your shooter but he's involved in something up to his neck. Good luck,' Gawn called after her as Rainey walked away.

Before she had a chance to say anything, Maxwell asked, 'What do you think about this drugs story, boss?'

'Drugs have come up a few times now, haven't they? Mostly to do with Nina but Dahlstrøm told me that Norrie was a user as well.'

'It kind of takes our case off in another direction, doesn't it?' Maxwell said.

'Maybe. Jack's already checked with the Drugs Squad. They couldn't suggest anyone capable of this. But, if they had crossed somebody, Norrie might have tried to talk their way out of trouble by making promises of a big pay-off from his father.'

Gawn was thinking on her feet. She wasn't sure she believed there was a link to drugs.

'By the way,' Maxwell said, 'I had a word with the sergeant in Carrick when I was out checking on the search. He knows Nabney and Nelson. He says they're OK. He told me there's the occasional bit of funny business in that area so the fishermen would be used to turning a blind eye. But they aren't involved in anything. He's confident of that.'

Gawn wasn't surprised or disappointed.

'If this is something to do with drugs, do you think any gang here would want to take diamonds for payment? How could they get rid of them?' Maxwell said, echoing her own doubts.

'Who knows what sort of connections they might have to fence diamonds? Check back with the Drugs Squad about that. For all we know, Norrie might have connections to get rid of the diamonds himself. It's probably worth asking Dahlstrøm about that too.'

'Tonight, you mean?' Maxwell asked, looking disappointed.

'Did you have something special on tonight, Inspector?'

'Well, yes. It's date night,' Maxwell said looking awkward, trying not to meet her eye.

'Date night?' Gawn repeated slowly.

'Kerri and I have a date night once a month. Time just for us now the kids are getting up a bit. "Reviving the romance," she says.' He sounded a little sceptical and a little embarrassed. 'She read about it in some magazine,' he added.

'Do you need to revive your romance?' Gawn asked and ostentatiously pulled a face at him.

'No. Of course not. It's just she'll be disappointed, that's all. It's usually a Friday night but I'd already changed it to tonight to leave tomorrow free with the deadline for the ransom coming up.'

'OK. Sian can talk to Dahlstrøm then. She's already spoken to him so he knows her and Jack can contact the Drugs Squad again. He has lots of mates there. Far be it from me to kill off romance, Paul. I wouldn't like to be responsible for a spike in the divorce rate among PSNI officers.'

'Aw, it's not like that, Gawn,' Maxwell said.

'I'm joking, Paul. Even cops are entitled to a private life. But I've always found a bottle of champagne and some sexy underwear was enough to revive the romance. You and Kerri should try that.'

Gawn smiled at the shocked look on Maxwell's face in reaction to her words. Then her voice changed. She sounded serious again. 'But we are against the clock. You know that. Warn Kerri not to expect you home tomorrow night. At all. This is the first real lead we've had apart from our theories that it has something to do with Nina's father and what he might have been involved in. That was a long time ago. It's probably not relevant. Who waits thirty years for payback? I'd speak to Dahlstrøm myself, but I have this bloody TV show to do.'

Gawn glanced at her watch.

'Hell. I'm going to be late.'

Chapter 57

Traffic was heavy. Heavier than she'd anticipated. Trying to find somewhere to park on the street was always going to be difficult.

She had followed the one-way system round Dublin Road and Great Victoria Street twice without success. Eventually she decided there was nothing for it but to try the multi-storey car park between the railway station and the Europa Hotel.

She found a space near the pedestrian exit and lifts on the very top level and manoeuvred her Porsche within its tight confines.

All her focus was on getting to the studio. She climbed out and reached back inside to get her briefcase. It was dark in the car so she had to search around to find the black briefcase lying on the black carpet behind the driver's seat.

Suddenly, she was grabbed from behind. She had heard other cars, but they had seemed far away on other levels, not up here. She hadn't heard a car door opening or a footstep behind her. But someone was suddenly right there, pulling her back out of the car. She was about to swing around and confront her attacker when an electric SUV, its engine almost silent, rounded the corner of the ramp at speed and came to a halt beside her. Two figures dressed totally in black jumped out. Her arms were pinioned behind her and her head was held, pressing her face against the car window so she couldn't move.

Gawn tried to steady her breathing and think. They must be carjackers. They must have followed her expensive car into the car park and now they were going to take it. It happened. She was insured. She'd let them take the car. It wasn't worth getting hurt to save it.

'Take the car. Just don't hurt me.'

Just then she felt a hand lifting her jacket and moving along the waistband of her trousers. Her initial horror was quickly replaced by shock as she realised her personal weapon was being lifted out of its holster. That was when she realised this was neither random nor opportunistic. They hadn't just happened on a lone woman in an expensive car. They had known she would be armed. They had known who she was.

Chapter 58

Relieved of her gun, the pressure on Gawn's arms was eased and the two men holding her from behind turned her around to face them and then let her go. They pushed her back roughly against her car.

She massaged her upper arms to show they had hurt her. They hadn't really. She had as much damage done to her at her self-defence classes. But she would play the frightened weak woman although, somehow, she didn't think they would be fooled. The only question was, what did they want with her?

Gawn could see her attackers face to face, but it didn't help. They were all wearing ski masks with slits for their eyes and their mouths. Two were tall, taller than her. Black trousers, black jackets – two in leather and one in a padded blouson style. None of them had spoken yet. One man was holding her gun in his hand.

'Take the car,' she said again, trying to sound frightened, which wasn't too difficult.

She was out of practice at this sort of thing. Not that you ever got used to the physical dangers you might encounter but she'd got soft. She felt naked without her weapon and, although she had the extending baton she always carried on duty, she didn't think she'd be able to get to it without them grabbing her again and stopping her. They could take it off her and beat her with it. Three against one were not good odds.

'We don't want your poncy car,' one of them said. His voice was gravelly as if he had a sore throat or was a heavy smoker. The other two laughed at his comment. 'We only want to give you a wee message, love.'

Gawn gritted her teeth. She thought of Mancarelli but it wasn't him. This man was taller and anyway Mancarelli was still in custody. If she got out of this with no more than having to endure being called 'love' by some hood, she'd do well.

'Tomorrow night. Midnight. Plot 134T.'

'What are you talking about?' she asked although she had recognised the number right away.

'Don't play games with me, love. You know what I'm talking about. *You* bring the diamonds.'

The speaker was moving her gun from hand to hand, almost as if it was just a child's toy and he was playing with it. The movement back and forth was almost mesmerising. She hoped he hadn't knocked the safety catch off by mistake. The stupid bastard could end up shooting himself or her.

'Leave the diamonds on the headstone.'

'What about Nina and Norrie?' Gawn asked. 'When do we get them back?'

She was amazed that her voice sounded so normal. Inside she was like a jelly. She needed to control her body. If they saw her shaking, they would enjoy reducing a DCI to a quivering mess.

'Don't worry, love. You'll get them back. In one piece, if you do what we say.'

The speaker laughed but there was no humour in the sound. It was cruel and she remembered the threat to send the hostages back piece by piece.

'One more thing,' the man said and tapped her gun on the roof of her car.

A frisson of fear shot through her body. Was the "one more thing" an attack to ensure she knew they meant business? She was already planning how to defend herself to minimise her injuries.

'We want you to include something in your TV interview tonight, love.'

They knew about the interview? They must have got their information from somewhere. But it hadn't been a secret she was going to take part. She'd complained enough about it. Most of her team had known. Gawn knew Maxwell had told his wife. People in McWilliams' office knew the details too and the staff on the show would have been given her name. Even Sebastian and his family could have passed it on. Someone had gossiped and word had got back to the kidnappers.

'Jacob's Island.'

Two words were all the man said and tapped the gun against the roof of her car again to emphasise them. What? She didn't understand. She thought she must have misheard. What sort of a message was Jacob's Island?

'Say it,' the man ordered and waved the gun inches away from her face.

'Jacob's Island,' she repeated quickly. 'What does it mean?' she asked.

'You don't need to fuckin' know what it means. You just need to say it, love. If you don't…' The man paused and nodded to one of the others.

He reached inside his jacket and withdrew a long-bladed knife. It looked very like the one Gawn and Maxwell had watched in the video of Nina. The man took a step nearer to her and sneezed loudly before he pointed the knife at Gawn's throat stopping within an inch of her skin so she could imagine the sensation of it pricking into her and drawing blood. She could imagine the red liquid trickling down her throat in a colourful rivulet staining her white shirt. She found herself wishing she was wearing a stab vest although it wouldn't really help her if he was going for her throat.

'My associate here will take great pleasure in sending Nina back to you one piece at a time.'

Just then they all heard the noise of an approaching car engine and all four heads turned in unison in the direction of the sound. Someone was on the level below and could be with them in seconds. The first man, the one holding her gun, nodded to the other two. They pushed her roughly back into her own car, slammed the door shut and then ran for their SUV which took off at speed. By the time she had managed to clamber back out of the Porsche, they were round the end of the exit ramp and out of sight.

Gawn was trembling. She reached down and lifted her service weapon off the ground. She saw it shaking in her hand. Thank God, they hadn't taken it. That would have jammed her up with red tape; it might have resulted in her being subjected to an internal investigation and taken off the case. At least for a while. She couldn't risk that.

She thought of the expensive watch she had noticed when the knifeman's sleeve had slipped up a little. She'd had a close view of it – too close – when he held the knife to her throat. She thought she had just met the man in the video who had cut Nina. Was he also the man who had shot Fraser?

Chapter 59

What should she do?

If she had got the car licence plate, she could have called it in. But the plate had been covered in mud – not by accident, she was sure - and she didn't even know what make the vehicle was. She'd only got a quick look at it. The men would be halfway up the Westlink and out of Belfast before they could get any cars out searching for them.

So what else? She could imagine the question being posed in some police recruitment or promotion test. She knew the answer. She should report what had happened, get a forensics team out, close the car park off and let them begin a fingertip search of the area around her car in case her attackers had dropped something or left some traces of themselves. The CSIs could fingerprint her car but all three men had been wearing gloves. She remembered their sinister-looking blue hands, covered in the same nitrile gloves that crime scene technicians wear to prevent contaminating scenes.

There was always the car park CCTV but the kidnappers had been wearing masks. They could start checking traffic cameras to find where the car had gone but she knew all about the problems with staffing now. Manpower was at a premium. She'd have to argue to have people pulled off other jobs to look for a black SUV with no number plate. Anyway, Gawn guessed the car was either straight onto a bonfire or into some breaker's yard where it would be in a hundred pieces before the morning. She'd get her own team to search the traffic cameras.

Gawn knew she wasn't going to do any of that. She had no desire to have a starring role on screen but she couldn't afford to miss this interview. If she didn't appear, they might panic and dispose of their two victims. She couldn't risk that.

The only thing that had been hurt in the encounter was her pride. She hadn't lost her weapon. They had barely even mussed her hair and anyway, she'd be getting her make-up done in the studio. She could do this.

In almost a dream-like state or maybe, more accurately, a nightmare state, she crossed the busy road and was buzzed into the TV studios.

'I'm here for *Crime Round-Up*,' Gawn told a young man sitting behind a counter when she walked into the reception area. It was the first time she had spoken since her encounter in the car park and she was pleased her voice sounded so normal.

'Name, please?' He looked up at her and asked.

'Gawn Girvin. Detective Chief Inspector Girvin.'

He laughed and his unexpected reaction drew a puzzled stare from her.

'Sorry. I must have misheard when I was taking down the list of guests for tonight's show. I was expecting a Dan Girvin,' he explained. 'Just take a seat, please.'

He motioned to a row of three tub chairs in front of a wall of photographs of people she recognised from local television programmes.

'One of the production assistants will be down in a minute to take you up to the studios,' the receptionist called across to her.

He smiled again somewhat apologetically at his earlier mistake about her name and then got back to work, answering a telephone call.

Gawn didn't have long to wait. A skinny girl dressed in jeans and an Aran sweater with the sleeves rolled up to reveal arms covered with colourful tattoos bounced through a set of swinging double doors just beside her.

'Hi there. I'm Julie. I'm a production assistant on *Crime Round-Up*. I'll take you upstairs now. Just follow me.'

She turned on her heel and pushed her way back through the doors letting them swing back on Gawn. Gawn knew she was late. Not by much, but TV had to work to deadlines and they would be rushing her through now.

'Sorry I'm late,' Gawn said. 'I had problems parking.'

Julie didn't comment. She just smiled and continued leading her through a rabbit warren of narrow windowless corridors, where they were flanked by rows of large, black and white publicity photographs of smiling men and women, only some of whom Gawn recognised. They passed doors with blacked-out glass sections in them and red or green lights over them, some illuminated.

'They'll be broadcasting the news from in there. It's just coming up to the time for the connection to London,' Julie explained, nodding in the direction of one of the doors they were passing. The light above it turned to red as they passed.

Gawn thought she would never be able to find her way back out. It was like a maze.

Eventually, Julie pushed against another set of double doors and they opened with a loud whoosh. Gawn found herself in an open-plan office reminiscent of her own incident room. There was that same sense of busyness. There were desks and computer screens and people working or standing together chatting over documents or munching on sandwiches. They all looked about twelve, Gawn thought to herself and suddenly felt old.

'This is Myra, our director.'

Julie introduced Gawn to a slim woman of about her own age with a pair of frameless glasses dangling from a chain around her neck and a harried expression on her face. Her greying hair gave her a more experienced look in comparison to the baby-faced Julie. Myra was clutching a clipboard and Gawn could see a sheet of paper covered in colour-coded rectangles and squiggles. Colour-coding must be a media thing, she guessed, remembering McWilliams' office with its folders.

'Welcome! Welcome, Gawn!'

Myra stepped forward as she spoke and, for just a second, Gawn thought she was going to hug her. Gawn flinched at Myra's pronunciation of her name.

'Thank you so much for coming,' Myra said with a harassed smile.

'Hi Myra,' Gawn said. 'My name is actually pronounced Gawn, you know, like Dan only with a *G*.'

She hoped Myra wouldn't take offence. She didn't.

'Thank you for telling me, Gawn. That would have been a bit of a disaster if we'd introduced you with the wrong name, wouldn't it?'

Myra laughed.

'First time on TV?' she added, any awkwardness overcome.

Gawn wondered if she looked so nervous and dumbstruck that the director was interpreting it as stage fright.

Myra sat her down on a hard grey plastic chair, handed her a cup of coffee in a paper cup – well, what could just about pass for coffee – and took her through the running order. Gawn would be given over to the care of the make-up artists next and then someone would check her clothes.

'Check my clothes?'

'Yes. Check how the colours look on camera, you know. We don't want you clashing with the presenters or disappearing into the green screen so you end up looking like a headless body.' Myra chuckled at the image she had conjured up for herself. 'We want you looking your best. And they'll check that your shirt or jacket don't need to be pressed. We're not going for the *Columbo* look.' The woman laughed at her own joke and tilted her head, reminding Gawn of Wilkinson.

'Your case is first on the running order,' she continued. 'That will give us plenty of time for callers.'

McWilliams had been right.

'Do you think you'll get any?' Gawn asked. She still had her doubts about the programme. It could be a massive waste of her time; time she could be putting to much better use.

'Oh, yes. There'll be some at least. We have our regulars who like to be helpful even if they haven't been within a hundred miles of anything. They phone in every programme.'

'We call that wasting police time,' Gawn offered.

Myra just chuckled. 'Ach, no. They're harmless and we have enough phonelines and people waiting to take messages that it won't stop any serious callers getting through. There could be some useful calls, you know. People who don't read the paper but watch us. People whose memory is jogged by something you might say. You could get something useful. Your colleagues have in the past, you know.'

'Ready?'

It was bouncy Julie, full of energy and enthusiasm, back again. Now she had a clipboard too and a stopwatch dangling round her neck to rival Myra's spectacles chain.

'Time for make-up, Gawn.'

Chapter 60

The next hour passed more quickly than Gawn expected or wanted. Every second was bringing her nearer her TV performance. She was dreading it and she still hadn't even met the presenters or been told exactly what questions she could expect to be asked.

Eventually they had finished poking and prodding her and she was waiting in the green room, her nerves jangling, more heavily made-up than she had ever been before. The chatty make-up artists had raved about her beautiful green eyes but said she looked rather pale and they'd added extra colour into her cheeks and a touch of eye shadow, something she seldom wore and never at work. Gawn wasn't surprised she looked pale even with the remnants of her Californian tan. They'd look pale too if they'd just been manhandled by three men in a dark car park.

Gawn had a glossy magazine sitting on her knee, closed now. She had flicked a few pages over in a desultory manner but she hadn't really looked at them. She couldn't concentrate on anything but the coming interview and delivering the ransom tomorrow night.

The door opened and a familiar face appeared. Barry Hunter. She recognised him instantly. His shock of seemingly untidy blond hair and his generous lips, as she had once read them described in a newspaper feature about him, were unmissable. He fronted *Crime Round-Up* along with Sarah Mullvenny, who was known for her hard-hitting journalism and exposés. She had won an award for a feature she'd written on an underage grooming ring operating out of Dublin and trying to expand into Belfast. She had a reputation for asking probing questions and Gawn hoped Hunter would be doing her interview.

'Hello, there.' Hunter greeted her like an old friend.

He stepped forward into the room and proffered his hand. It felt soft and flabby to her touch.

'Thank you so much for taking part in the programme, Chief Inspector.'

As if she'd had any choice, she thought to herself.

There was just a hint of transatlantic accent in his speech. He hailed from Holywood, she knew. Holywood, County Down, not California.

Gawn had to make the right noises. McWilliams would expect it. So would Wilkinson and the chief constable. PR was important and the PSNI didn't always hit the headlines for the right reasons.

'No. Thank you, Barry, for the chance to talk about my case.'

Hunter sat down beside her on the plush sofa although there were two vacant chairs in the small room that he could have chosen.

'I'll be interviewing you this evening, Gawn,' he said.

Gawn sighed with relief, both that he'd got her name right and that she wasn't going to be facing Mullvenny. But the sigh had been louder than she'd intended, and she hoped he didn't misinterpret it as a response from an adoring fan.

Hunter sat with her for ten minutes, oozing charm the whole time. He went through some lines of questioning and the types of ways he would phrase his questions. It all sounded reasonable; doable. She thought she could cope with it.

'I like to keep it real. Keep it fluid. I don't work well to a script, which drives poor old Myra wild.' He smiled almost conspiratorially at her. 'There'll be an autocue to try to keep me in check, but I warn you, I may veer off it, if I find your answer particularly interesting or I feel it needs clarification for our viewers.'

If he could veer off topic, then so could she. She would just have to work the kidnapper's phrase in somehow, even if it did make her sound crazy.

'You're needed on set,' Julie said to Hunter, poking her head round the doorframe.

'I'll see you down there, Gawn.'

Hunter smiled at her one last time, patted her on the shoulder and walked out. Gawn was left alone to contemplate her fate.

But not for long. Julie reappeared.

'Ready? We're waiting for you, Gawn. Showtime.'

This was it.

Chapter 61

Her interview flew by.

Afterwards she wouldn't have been able to say exactly what she had been asked or what she had answered.

As soon as she had walked into the studio, she'd been aware of the heat emanating from the banks of lights hanging down overhead. They were almost blinding, making it impossible to see beyond a few metres. She hoped she didn't look like a rabbit caught in the headlights or too sweaty under the heat they were producing.

Almost before she had got into her stride talking about Nina and Norrie and asking for witnesses to come forward, it seemed to be over and she was being chivvied off set by Julie.

'Great job! You did really well.'

Gawn reckoned she would say that anyway to everybody. No matter what they'd been like.

'Have a drink. Relax. You can watch the rest of the show.'

There was a TV screen mounted on the wall in the Green room. It had been blank earlier when she'd been waiting here. Now it was showing Sarah Mullvenny talking to camera and clips of the aftermath of yet another ATM theft.

There was a hospitality table in the corner with bottled water and facilities to make tea or coffee in a little hot drinks machine too.

She tried to watch the programme but the sound was turned down so she couldn't really hear. Anyhow, she needed time to think. She hadn't managed to use the kidnappers' phrase during the interview. There'd been no opportunity to slip it in. If she'd tried, she would have sounded like a complete idiot and Hunter might have picked up on it.

She had one more chance when they called her back down. It would only be a sentence or two. It was right at the end of the programme, but it should be enough to let her say the phrase and ensure no comment could be made about it afterwards. At least not on air.

Then a horrific thought struck her. What if Hunter went off script? He'd told her that sometimes he did that. She thought of Julie, stopwatch in hand, timing everything to the second. It was a live programme. It couldn't overrun. What if he used up too much time and they cut her final appearance? What if she didn't get the chance to speak again? What if she'd blown it for Nina and Norrie?

If they turned up dead, no one would know it was her fault. Except her, of course. No one else knew about the kidnappers' demand and they might kill the two hostages anyway. They might already have done it, for all she knew.

'Ready, Gawn? Ready for the big finale?' Julie said and smiled.

Thank God. She was going to get the chance to do it.

Chapter 62

There was no hesitation in Gawn's step. She practically ran down the narrow corridor to the studio. It was Julie who was tripping along in her wake trying to keep up.

Julie gave her a thumbs-up sign and then guided her into position at a table for two on one side of the studio while the cameras were focused on Barry Hunter at the other. He was standing in front of a green screen, talking and pointing to nothing as far as Gawn could see. When she glanced up at the monitor hanging overhead, she saw he looked as if he was standing in front of a changing array of photographs of wanted villains on the run and suspects the police were seeking to question.

A sound engineer appeared by her side and adjusted her microphone, rearranging her collar. Then, one of the make-up girls she'd met earlier replaced him and dabbed some powder on her face.

'We don't want you shining too brightly on camera,' she joked and turned away.

Behind the make-up girl, Sarah Mullvenny had slipped silently into the other chair at the table. She glanced up from her script and smiled at Gawn.

She mouthed, 'Great job. Just a couple of minutes.'

Gawn could feel her palms go sweaty. She had to get this right. This was her one and only chance. She couldn't just blurt out 'Jacob's Island'. She needed to make it sound as natural as possible so people wouldn't think anything about it. Well, most people anyway. She had worked out it would mean something important to someone. The kidnappers were trying to get a message out. But what message? And to whom?

Gawn was jerked out of her thoughts as Mullvenny introduced her.

'We have DCI Gawn Girvin back with us to hear about the response to her appeal about two missing tourists.'

Mullvenny's voice was velvety smooth with a slight D4 accent and no sign of nerves. This was her métier. She was at home in front of the cameras. She swivelled just a fraction in her seat so she could still be seen on camera but was looking directly at Gawn.

'We've had a really good response to the story of your . two missing tourists, Chief Inspector,' the journalist began.

Her missing tourists, Gawn registered. They were her missing tourists. Except Gawn wasn't sure how "missing" one was. But they were "hers".

'We've had reports of sightings all along the North Coast. People have been phoning in from Portrush to Derry and even into Donegal. I presume you'll be following up on these,' Mullvenny asked and leaned forward in an almost exaggerated manner encouraging Gawn to respond.

'Yes, of course, Sarah,' Gawn said jauntily and smiled in what she hoped was a professional but friendly manner as if she and Sarah were chatting casually. She glanced away from Mullvenny to smile directly into the camera too.

'And there's one here from a viewer in Dublin,' the presenter said glancing down at her notes. 'Have you considered they might have gone back south of the border? That was the way they arrived in Northern Ireland, wasn't it?' she asked and waited as if she'd asked something clever.

As if they hadn't considered that straight away, Gawn thought, but made sure her thoughts were not reflected on her face.

'We're not ruling anything out at this stage, Sarah. We're checking border crossings, airports, ferry ports all over the island of Ireland and campsites, of course. But we're very excited that we've had a suggestion they might have been seen at Jacob's Island. We'll be following up on that too.'

Gawn could see the puzzled expression that suddenly appeared on Mullvenny's face. The woman was scrutinising the sheet of paper in her hand. She was surprised at Gawn's mention of Jacob's Island. Gawn thought she'd probably have wanted to ask a follow-up question about it if there'd been time. But, professional that she was, she disguised all that and moved on without comment. She thanked Gawn effusively and all the other contributors to the programme and then left her to walk across and join Hunter at the other side of the studio for their signature farewell.

* * *

'Jacob's Island. Where's that? We didn't get any calls about a sighting at Jacob's Island, did we, Julie? I've never heard of the place.'

Mullvenny had directed her question to Julie who had abandoned her stopwatch and was visibly more relaxed, now the show was finished. Myra appeared behind her.

'Did we, Myra?' Mullvenny asked, joining the producer in the conversation.

'Did we what?' Myra asked having missed the start of what was being said.

'Get a call from someone suggesting the police look at Jacob's Island.'

Myra scanned down the page on her clipboard, her eyes following her finger down the page.

'It's not on my list,' she answered.

Mullvenny turned to Gawn. The sound engineer was busy removing the microphone from her collar, hiding her from the presenter's stare.

Gawn thought she better offer some explanation. It wasn't beyond the bounds of possibility that an experienced journalist like Mullvenny might get suspicious and take it into her head to do some digging, sensing a story.

'No. I got a call about it,' Gawn said.

She hoped there was no way they could know she was lying. Then she realised phone calls might be blocked inside the studio. She added, 'I went outside for a minute to cool down and my sergeant phoned me. I thought it might be worthwhile mentioning it in case it jogged anyone's memory. I know you keep your lines open for another hour and you gave out the police number too so someone might ring us direct. I've never heard of Jacob's Island either. I don't even know where it is.'

This was true. She was hoping Mullvenny wouldn't check up on her story. There would be a log for entries and exits to the building. She couldn't just have wandered out.

'I hoped someone might react and let us know or verify that Nina and Norrie had been there or maybe they still are there blissfully unaware of all the fuss. I'm presuming it's some spot where people like to wild camp. It's probably somewhere in the back of beyond with no internet access,' she added. 'I'll be following up on it, you can be sure.'

Gawn was worried. She was blabbering now. Mullvenny might smell a rat. She just wanted to get away. She'd done what had been asked of her by both McWilliams and the kidnappers. Now she needed to get back to work.

Just over twenty-four hours to go.

Chapter 63

The air outside was cool but that was welcome. Tiny droplets of rain hit against her cheeks. It had been hot and stuffy in the studios. Gawn took a deep breath. The fumes of taxis and cars idling on the roadway, waiting for pickups from pubs and the nearby theatre, filled her nostrils but she didn't mind. It was just good to be outside and away from any awkward questions.

It had been daylight when she went into the building. Now it got dark, there was a different side to Belfast. Nightlife, pubs, clubs, boozy groups of stags or hens on party bikes downing their drinks and yahooing as they passed by. The streetlights were reflected in pools of water lying by the side of the road, a sign it had been raining heavily while she'd been indoors. A minibus passed at speed throwing up a wave of water onto the pavement. A homeless woman was standing just in front of Gawn. She was carrying her belongings in a rolled-up sleeping bag.

She jumped back just saving her feet and legs from a soaking.

'Bastards,' the woman yelled after it and shook her fist.

Gawn began walking purposefully towards the pedestrian crossing in front of The Crown bar. She wasn't looking forward to going inside the car park again.

There was already a group of people waiting for the traffic lights to change. Before she reached them, she became aware of two men, one on either side of her. They were well-dressed business types, wearing dark suits and overcoats. They had her hemmed in between them, invading her personal space, almost shoulder to shoulder with her like a file of soldiers on parade.

It might just be chance. Perhaps the men were simply walking along the crowded pavement. But she didn't think so. They were keeping in step with her. Once she slowed down slightly and they did too, keeping pace.

Were the kidnappers back? Had she served her purpose now? She had delivered their message so were they going to finish the job they had started in the car park, in case she could somehow recognise them?

As she came to Amelia Street on her right, Gawn made a move. She barged against the man on her inside, shoulder charging him and pushing him into a group of noisy young people behind them. She took off down the dark side street. It would give her a head start. Not much of one, but a little.

As she ran, Gawn could hear running footsteps behind her. She didn't look round, that would slow her down, but she could hear them following her. If she could just reach the elbow bend in the street, there was a popular bar there. She could go inside, mingle with the crowd and phone for reinforcements. But, before she got that far, a man stepped out of a long black limousine parked on her side of the street. It could be another coincidence, but she didn't think so. All her senses were heightened. The following footsteps were gaining on her. She cursed her high-heel shoes.

The man, dressed in a dark suit and wearing a cap, was standing in the middle of the pavement blocking her way. Just then the back door of the car opened and a voice boomed out from within.

'Good evening, Chief Inspector.'

Her two pursuers had reached her and one held the car door open for her until she got into the back seat. Sir Patrick Montgomery was sitting there. As soon as she was settled, the car moved off.

Chapter 64

'You've been looking for me,' Montgomery said.

Gawn wondered how he had heard. Had Matt Lynch or Mike Lee told him or had he heard about their inquiries?

'Where are we going?' she asked, ignoring his words of greeting and looking out of the darkened car window at the passing streetscape.

'Nowhere in particular. I just don't want to attract the attention of any of your colleagues, that's all. I've told my driver to take us on a little tour of the city so we can talk without any interruptions.

'Amelia Street used to have a certain reputation, you know,' he continued, 'and a car sitting waiting with a lone man in it who is then joined by a younger woman might be misinterpreted.'

Even with only the dim light that was filtering into the vehicle from the passing streetlights, she could see he was almost smiling at her. The smile reminded her of a snake.

Gawn didn't think she was in any danger from Montgomery. She had met men like him before. They were cold and calculating but she didn't think she posed any threat to him nor he to her.

This part of the city was always busy. She knew where she was but not where she was going, or where this conversation was headed. They were passing pubs and clubs and restaurants, some with queues outside. It was a main thoroughfare from the university quarter into the city centre favoured by raucous groups of students, heading for a good night out. There would be regular police patrols on the lookout for trouble.

'You don't need to protect my reputation, Sir Patrick,' she said.

'It's not your reputation I was thinking of, my dear.'

Being called 'my dear' by someone who didn't even know her was only marginally less annoying than being called 'love'. But then she realised Montgomery did know her. At least he must know a lot about her.

He swivelled in his seat so he was looking directly at her. They were side by side. He was a big man and he took up more than half the bench seat. Gawn moved away slightly, trying to put some distance between them. She leant back against the car door and fixed him with a stare.

'You were trying to contact me, so I've been told, Chief Inspector.'

It was a statement and a question.

'Yes. I was. I am. I didn't think there was any point in talking to my boss or even to the chief constable. You're the one who knows what's going on with Nina and Norrie.'

'I assure you I have no idea where the two young folk are.'

Montgomery was shaking his head from side to side. Gawn believed him.

'If I did, I would have told your chief constable and had them rescued. Jorgen Pedersen is a very old and good friend of mine. I hate to think what he and his dear wife are going through waiting for news.'

'But he's not the only reason you're involved in this case, is he?'

Montgomery didn't answer.

'I know this has something to do with Alan Phillips and Denton Fraser.'

She had dropped the names like bombs into her sentence. She watched carefully for Montgomery's reaction. His face remained almost impassive. Only a flicker of his eyelids betrayed him. He ran his tongue over his lips. This was the first sign of weakness she had seen in him. In police headquarters he had seemed a man in total control of himself and everyone around him. Now he seemed slightly unsure. She had hit a nerve. She was right.

Gawn moved in for the kill.

'And, my father,' she added.

Chapter 65

Montgomery's head jerked up immediately at the mention of Gawn's father. She had surprised him by the fact she knew there was some connection between all three men. She waited in silence while Montgomery picked at an imaginary mark on his trouser leg.

Eventually he said in a steady, toneless voice, 'You have been a busy bee, haven't you? I was warned, you know.'

He swiped something off his leg, reminding Gawn of someone swatting an insect away. It was probably what he would like to do to her at the minute. A busy bee he had called her. He'd probably like to get rid of her like some annoying insect too.

'Warned?'

'That I wouldn't be able to control you if you got started on this case. I was advised someone else would be more *appropriate*,' he told her, enunciating the word slowly.

'Appropriate?'

Montgomery didn't react. She needed to exploit any advantage she had from surprising him. He would gather himself again and close down her questions if she didn't press ahead now.

'Alan Phillips is Nina's father, isn't he? He disappeared from Belfast in 1995. I presume everyone was meant to think he was dead. But he isn't or, at least, he wasn't,' Gawn said.

She knew she wasn't telling him anything he didn't already know and his emotionless expression confirmed that for her. His face was a blank mask. He was silent for a few seconds then he began speaking in a low voice which was controlled but hinted at displeasure.

'Yes. He is her father,' Montgomery admitted. 'Nina, or Eileen I suppose I should call her, must have tracked him down. God knows how. Perhaps he contacted her. I don't know. He was always a doting father and the only demand he made before helping us was that she would always be safe and well looked after.

'I made sure she was. I'm a man of my word, Chief Inspector. I knew Eileen had ended up in Oslo last year. I'd kept an eye on her. I rekindled my old friendship with Pedersen so I could visit the city and see her for myself. I never contacted her directly. I wasn't sure how much her mother had told her.

'But it seems Marie must have told her all about her father, which I think is why she left home and went a bit wild. Wanting to talk to him once she knew he was alive must have got her started searching for him. Or maybe being out of contact might have got too much for him in the end. It's nearly thirty years ago. I suppose he thought he was safe. Or he got careless.'

'People have long memories. Especially people here,' Gawn said. 'We're still fighting over things that happened three hundred years ago. What exactly did Phillips do for you?'

'Phillips was a nobody. Just an ordinary working man. He'd got sucked into the edges of a gang. Not terrorists. I believe they are normally referred to nowadays as OCGs. He owed them money for bits of furniture, would you believe? Not drugs or anything criminal like that. He'd borrowed the money to furnish his house. It was rather touching actually.

'They asked him to help them with something they needed to pay off his debt. He was an engineer. He stole some parts from his work and passed them on. That was all. A bomb was built, and his fingerprints were on the components.'

'And you turned him? You used him against them?'

'Yes,' Montgomery said. 'We were able to identify where the parts had come from and trace them back to him. It was relatively simple to convince him to give evidence against the gang.'

His tone was matter-of-fact. Gawn realised he would be making no excuses for what he had done.

'Who were you? Who are you?' Gawn asked.

'I am who I say I am. I'm with the ministry now trying my best to boost Britain's trade but I was in military intelligence back then. A fairly lowly lieutenant who got the dirty jobs. I was leading a joint operation with the RUC. We knew both sides were making use of criminal gangs and there was the suspicion that some members of the RUC might be involved. There was a lot of dirty dealing going on. Money changing hands. I was working with an undercover team.'

Gawn felt her blood run cold.

'You thought my father was part of that? You thought he was a dirty cop?'

Chapter 66

'No. No, my dear. Your father was part of the small RUC undercover group working with my team. He and his partner had infiltrated the gangs. They were killed because they were getting too close to somebody. Someone recognised them. They were unlucky. Their cover was blown.'

'But they were in uniform on patrol when they were killed,' Gawn said. 'It was terrorists.'

'Come, come, Chief Inspector. Do you seriously think it was beyond the scope of counter-intelligence to interfere with the evidence? They were neither in uniform nor on patrol. They had a meeting set up with some of the gang. It was a trap. When they were killed, we needed to ensure our other assets weren't compromised too and that word didn't get back before we could make arrests. It was easy enough to make it seem like another terrorist attack.'

'Assets?'

That's all her father had been to this man?

'Your father died a hero and was buried as such. Full honours. It made no difference if he was in uniform at the time or not. It wouldn't have helped your mother or you or Constable Dalton's family either to know any of that. The cover-up allowed us to extricate our assets so they could give evidence in court.'

'Like Phillips?'

'Yes, like Phillips. His evidence helped us put some seriously dangerous men behind bars.'

Montgomery was right of course. It wouldn't have lessened the loss her mother had felt for the rest of her life. Her father was a hero whether he'd been killed out on patrol or doing undercover work. But it seemed the past had now come back to haunt them all.

'So what do the kidnappers want? What do they hope to gain by grabbing Nina and Norrie?' Gawn asked.

'Norrie, I suspect, nothing. He's just collateral damage and I'm rather afraid that makes him disposable, but Nina, that's different. They obviously want to draw Phillips out into the open and holding his daughter is the way they hope to do it. Whoever they are,' Montgomery said.

'You don't know?' Gawn asked.

'There were several gangs we were trying to break up as a way to lessen their influence in parts of Belfast and prevent further deaths,' Montgomery continued. 'We needed evidence against them and against the men in the shadows who were behind them. It could be someone from any one of the gangs or even some of the people who were on the take at the time. We never identified them. Your father came close, I think. Too close probably. Some of those people might still be around now with a lot to lose.'

'What about Fraser? How does he fit in?' Gawn asked, although she thought she knew the answer.

'He was working for us too. He had a few nasty habits and we were able to convince him to help us out in return for keeping his dirty little secrets quiet.'

'You blackmailed him?' Gawn asked.

'It was a dirty business. I'm not proud of some of the things I had to do but I am proud of what we achieved. Most people here are enjoying the benefits.'

Gawn wasn't sure whether she was being told the truth. Montgomery wasn't going to apologise for what he had done.

'Fraser passed on information,' Montgomery continued. 'Someone must have worked that out. He was probably killed because he wouldn't talk and give Phillips up – he couldn't, he didn't know. Phillips slipped out of sight years ago. Even I don't know where he is.'

Chapter 67

Friday

'You were attacked… in the multi-storey car park in Great Victoria Street?'

She hadn't told Sebastian what had happened. He had been cock-a-hoop about her TV appearance. He'd had a bottle of champagne chilling in the fridge and was ready to celebrate with her. She had pleaded a headache and gone straight to bed but not before phoning Maxwell and telling him to meet her in the office at 6am.

She had just started to tell her inspector everything that had happened.

'You weren't hurt?' Maxwell asked.

'No. They didn't want to hurt me. They just wanted their message out there and they needed me as their mouthpiece.'

'"Jacob's Island". What does it mean?' he asked.

'I presume it's a place. Put everybody you can spare onto finding out where it is. It could be where Nina and Norrie are being held, though I don't know why the kidnappers would give that away.'

Gawn suspected she did know but she wasn't ready to share that with Maxwell just yet.

'But the bottom line is, we need to find it. Fast. And get someone to get hold of yesterday's CCTV from the car park and have a look for the SUV. I doubt it will help much, but who knows?'

'Dahlstrøm phoned yesterday after you left, boss, to say Pedersen has the diamonds and he's flying in first thing this morning. He should be here soon,' he said looking at his watch.

'We'll need to get them from him. The kidnappers want *me* to deliver the ransom, not him. This is a map of the Lambeg area. The graveyard where they want me to leave the diamonds is here,' she said.

Gawn had opened a folded Ordnance Survey map, smoothing it out over her desk and moving her cup and a pile of papers out of the way.

'It's very open country, mostly isolated farmhouses until you get to the outskirts of Lisburn.'

Maxwell could see that for himself. There were few buildings in the vicinity of the graveyard, other than the church.

'It was a good spot for them to pick,' she said. 'Good for them, I mean,' she added, seeing his expression. 'They obviously wanted to involve me because of my father and his connection to Phillips. They want me there, where my father's buried.'

She had already shared some of what Montgomery had told her with Maxwell and sworn him to secrecy. At least for now. How much of the back story would come out in the end, how much would be allowed to come out, she didn't know. But she couldn't expect Maxwell to work in the dark and, anyway, she needed to trust someone.

'It's going to be difficult to position anyone to keep watch without being seen. The nearest house is probably about a quarter of a mile away and it doesn't have a direct view,' Maxwell said, pointing to the map.

'We could get someone into the church tower if we move quickly, Paul. They'd have a three-hundred-and-sixty-degree view from there and with a nightscope it'd be perfect. They'd see everything for miles around, not just in the churchyard. They could monitor the whole area.

'Get in touch with the vicar. Give him just enough information to ask if we can put an officer there overnight. Then contact the ARU and get someone. Their best shot.'

'You're not going to try to put anyone in the churchyard?' Maxwell asked, looking worried.

'Where? Lurking behind the gravestones like a bunch of zombies?'

Gawn immediately thought of Magwitch in the Dickens novel.

'For all we know, the kidnappers are already watching. I don't know from where but they could be. They'd notice if a whole lot of people started disappearing in the graveyard, wouldn't they? Anyway, I don't think I'm their target. I don't think I'll be in any danger. If they'd wanted to kill me, they could have done it last night.'

As Gawn spoke, she realised they'd needed her last night. After she'd delivered the diamonds, they wouldn't need her anymore. She looked at Maxwell and knew he was thinking the same thing.

Chapter 68

She was swimming. But it was getting harder and harder to breath. The water was almost black beneath her and so, so cold. She was in one of the lochs where she and Norrie had spent time when they were in Scotland. She didn't know which one but she could see the hills all around her, rising up majestically into a grey sky. They really were covered in purple heather. But where was Norrie? She couldn't see him anywhere.

Nina was shivering uncontrollably.

'God, look at the state the bastard's left you in.'

It was a kindly voice, but it wasn't Norrie. A hand lifted her head and she felt an arm under her legs as she was scooped up and carried across the room. It was Doc, for she had opened her eyes and realised she was back in her prison and this wasn't Norrie. He set her down gently on top of some hay bales. He placed a blanket over her and tucked her in as she remembered her father doing. The blanket smelt of horses but she didn't care.

'Listen, love, you're going to have to trust me or you'll never get out of this alive. I didn't sign up for all this. It was supposed to be just grabbing you and your boyfriend, dumping him somewhere and keeping you here for a few days until they got what they wanted. This lot are fuckin' crazy. You don't deserve this.'

Nina didn't understand his words, but she felt warmer and somehow safer. Doc was going to save her. She didn't know how. She closed her eyes and drifted off back to her dreamland.

Doc didn't know either. But he did know he didn't want to be responsible for this girl's death.

Chapter 69

'Are you sure I can't do this? He is my son, Chief Inspector. I should be delivering the ransom.'

Pederson's face was lined with worry. He seemed to have aged years since she had seen him just a few days ago.

'They were very specific, Mr Ambassador. They said I was to bring the diamonds,' Gawn said.

The Norwegian was sitting, transferring a small purple velvet bag from one hand to the other in an unconscious nervous movement, reminding Gawn of the kidnapper's actions with her gun.

'Why you, Chief Inspector? I could do it if they don't want the ambassador involved,' Dahlstrøm offered.

He was standing behind the ambassador's chair almost like a bodyguard. There was one million pounds worth of diamonds in the room. He probably did feel protective of both them and his employer.

Gawn wasn't about to share what she knew with these men.

'They'll have read my name in the press or seen me on TV last night. That must have given them the idea,' she explained.

'But you're an experienced police officer. Wouldn't it be easier for them to deal with… an amateur, a worried father?' Dahlstrøm asked.

He had paused before calling Pedersen 'an amateur' but Gawn knew he was right of course. Without knowing everything that was going on, choosing her to deliver the ransom would seem strange. It was strange if you didn't know about the connection to her father.

'It's better all round, I assure you. I'll be in constant radio contact with my team. I'll have men in position ready to move in when the kidnappers come to pick up the diamonds. We'll get them and we'll get your son and his girlfriend.'

She hoped she sounded confident. She believed this wasn't really about diamonds. They were an added bonus for the kidnappers. It wasn't even about Norrie or Pedersen. And she wasn't sure if the kidnappers would kill the two hostages when they got what they wanted. Which wasn't the diamonds. It was Phillips. He was the ransom.

Chapter 70

Ballyskeagh Road was almost deserted. The poor weather seemed to have kept most people at home. It had been raining heavily earlier and the road surface was slippery, sparkling under the LED headlights of her new Cayenne, reminding Gawn of the diamonds sitting beside her in the little purple velvet bag on the passenger seat.

She had seen only one other vehicle, coming in the opposite direction, since she had turned onto this narrower road away from the bright lights of Belfast. The car's headlights had momentarily blinded her as she had rounded a tight corner on the windy back road to Lisburn. There were few houses and none were showing lights. It was as if the whole world was asleep, oblivious to the drama unfolding.

In Belfast there had been more traffic but she didn't think she had been followed. Why would the kidnappers need to follow her? They knew where she was going. Then a thought struck her. What if they planned to stop her and take the diamonds enroute before she got to the churchyard? That thought worried her but only for a second. No, she was sure they wanted to do the handover at the graveyard. It had a significance for them. And for her.

Now, on the little back road, she was sure she wasn't being followed. Concentrating on the road ahead, she drove quickly but carefully. She loosened her hold on the steering wheel. She realised she had been clutching it tightly, her knuckles white.

She had an armed officer in the church tower. They had been lucky. There had been a funeral that afternoon and the ARU officer had been able to go inside among the mourners and climb the tower into position. She didn't think the kidnappers would have been counting all the mourners in and out. They weren't that good. She hoped. But perhaps they had people hidden too. She had to consider that. So far, Tower 1, the call sign for the officer hidden in the church, was reporting all clear. No movement in the graveyard.

She was on her own. Her position was being tracked and she had her radio and her personal protection weapon as well as the expandable baton she always carried on callouts. It had proved its worth more than once. Unfortunately, not in the multi-storey car park. She would have liked to have been able to use it then.

Maxwell was keeping in constant contact. She knew cars would be waiting nearby too, hopefully where they would not be noticed, but ready to sweep in as soon as anything happened or to follow anyone coming to retrieve the ransom. She hadn't been able to risk deploying the police helicopter. On a still night like tonight, the sound of its rotors would have been too obvious echoing over the sleeping landscape and warning the kidnappers of its presence. It would have scared them off and they might have killed the hostages and run. Anyway, the cloud cover was probably too low for safe flying.

Would one of the kidnappers show up himself to take the diamonds from her? Would she get the chance to confront him? Probably not. They had said to leave the bag with the diamonds on top of the headstone, her father's headstone. That was no coincidence.

Were they just planning to walk in and lift it sometime later? Surely they knew that, once she left, the cemetery would be under observation. How did they expect to get away with it? That's what was worrying her. They could take her as a hostage to ensure safe passage for themselves and the ransom. If that happened, she had given a strict order for no one to intervene. They were to follow the diamonds back to the hostages no matter what.

Other worrying questions came into her mind. Was she a target for them too? Did they intend to grab her? Or perhaps to kill her as payback for what her father had been doing? Had she been part of the ransom all along, like Phillips?

Then she saw it. The old parish church suddenly appeared before her in a black silhouette against a dark sky with the moon peeping out from behind clouds. It stood on a rise overlooking the road, solid and almost menacing like some gothic edifice. The security lights in the delivery area of a local factory shone out from across the fields almost like an alien landing spot. But all was in darkness here.

Gawn drew her car to the side of the road, shut off the engine and took the little velvet bag from the passenger seat. She put it into her pocket and tapped it, almost as if she was reassuring herself it was there.

'I'm going into the graveyard now,' she said into her radio.

'Copy that, boss,' Maxwell's disembodied voice replied. He didn't tell her 'Good luck'. She hadn't expected him to. But she could hear the tension in his voice.

She stepped out of the car. A wall of silence hit her. Not even an owl was hooting. The factory in the distance might be well-lit but there was no noise coming from its machinery and the lorries which delivered to it 24/7 were not moving.

The lych-gate was locked. A heavy padlock was holding it together. She had expected that. Maxwell had told the vicar it was important he behaved exactly as usual. He was to lock up as he always did. The church wasn't really concerned about keeping people out of its grounds. It was too far away from the usual haunts of local youths to attract much vandalism. On either side of the wooden structure, sturdy stone walls enclosed the area but only at a little over waist height. Gawn was able to scale the wall with ease, landing on the grass on the other side and making her way to the main path between the rows of graves.

Her father's grave was at the top of the cemetery near the fence among the less recent interments. Crunch. Crunch. Crunch. Her steady footsteps sounded loud on the gravel pathway signalling her movements to anyone that might be listening.

Gawn scanned from left to right as she walked, using a heavy rubber torch that could double as a weapon if necessary. Tall headstones, some covered in lichen and moss, the writing on them almost worn away by a combination of age and weather, loomed up on either side of her. She could make out bouquets of flowers lying forlornly on one of the nearest graves and felt a pang of guilt at how seldom she had made this journey to visit her father's grave or leave flowers in his memory.

She wondered if she was being watched. She knew the officer in the tower would have her in his sights, but someone could be hidden behind one of the headstones invisible to her in the darkness. She felt strangely vulnerable. The hairs on the back of her neck rose at the scream of an animal, perhaps a fox, somewhere nearby. It had sounded almost human.

Suddenly, there it was, right in front of her.

In memory of Sergeant David Alexander Girvin (RUC), murdered in the line of duty.

It gave the date of her father's death and other details. She didn't read it. She didn't need to. She didn't need it written in stone. For her it was written in blood. Her father's blood.

Gawn fingered the little pouch in her pocket reassured by the sensation of the soft velvet material. The diamonds felt like a collection of worthless stones. She took the bag out of her pocket and set it on top of the headstone, careful to centre it so it wouldn't fall off into the long grass.

For a second, she wondered if she should take a moment to show her respect to her father, but she didn't. Placing the diamonds here was no mark of respect.

Her father would understand if she didn't take time, bow her head, say a prayer. He had taught her the value of duty. She wasn't here for him. Not this time. She would be back.

Gawn turned and walked quickly to her car without a backward glance.

Chapter 71

Saturday

The waiting had begun. Pedersen had kept his side of the bargain, providing the diamonds for the ransom. Gawn had kept hers, delivering them as they had asked. Now all they could do was wait. The kidnappers had not said when or where Nina and Norrie would be returned. Or in what condition.

It was nearly 3am. What were they waiting for? Maxwell suggested that perhaps the kidnappers would wait until daylight when they would be able to see any police cars in the vicinity. Or perhaps the ransom had never really been important to them. Gawn was beginning to suspect that more and more. Getting the diamonds had never been their object.

Gawn and Maxwell were sitting at DC Sharma's desk in the incident room. Maxwell's jacket was off and his tie was loosened. The top button of his shirt was undone. He looked fidgety and uncomfortable. He was holding a pen between the fingers of one hand, almost like a cigarette, and tapping it on the knuckles of the other.

Gawn had rolled her shirt sleeves up, ready for action except there wasn't any action to take. She was sitting on the edge of her chair bent over like a coiled spring, tension visible on every line of her face. Her fingers were tapping out an angry rhythm on her knee almost in time with Maxwell's pen and her legs were jiggling. The three, now-empty cups which had contained strong coffee had provided her with enough caffeine to have her bouncing off the ceiling.

The others were waiting too. Few were doing any real work, glancing at paperwork, checking an entry on their computer screen. Really they were all just waiting. Some of them weren't even supposed to be on duty but they'd wanted to hang around to hear the hostages' fate.

The phone rang and Jack Dee was quickest to get to it, jumping up out of his seat like a Jack-in-the-box. The room fell silent and eight pairs of ears strained to hear what the caller on the other end of the line was saying to Dee.

He listened carefully and then turned to address the DCI.

'They've spotted someone heading to the graveyard. Tower 1 just called it in,' Dee said. 'One figure. Coming over the fields.' He looked at Gawn, waiting for an order.

She hesitated.

'They want to know what to do, ma'am. Should they move in?'

Gawn and Maxwell exchanged a look.

'Tell them to hold back and watch until they're certain it's one of the kidnappers and not just somebody taking a shortcut over the fields after a night out. When he's right at the grave so they're absolutely certain, then they move in and follow. Do not intercept. Just follow. We can't lose him. He's our only connection to Nina and Norrie,' she said and stood up. 'I'm going back to the church, Paul. We mustn't lose him.'

Gawn sounded worried. She was worried. If they lost this man, they were back to square one. No one had been able to find Jacob's Island. Anywhere. It wasn't on any map. It must be some name familiar only to locals and that meant it could be anywhere.

* * *

Gawn hadn't quite reached Lambeg when Maxwell radioed to her.

'They've moved in on the figure in the graveyard.'

'What! I gave an order he was to be followed. Why did they stop him?' Gawn asked.

'It was a *her*,' Maxwell said.

'Her? One of the kidnappers is a woman?'

She was sure the three who had accosted her in the car park had all been men. There must be at least four in the gang then, if a woman had come to pick up the ransom. Perhaps it had been a woman who had taken the first ransom message to London while Dee had been searching for a man.

'No. It was Nina,' he told her. 'She collapsed. That's why they moved in. The paramedics have just arrived. They're taking her to the RVH.'

'Nina was picking up the ransom? Was she one of the kidnappers all along? Was it all a con, Paul?'

'No. She wasn't in a fit state to be questioned, according to Sharma. He's going with her in the ambulance.'

'I'll meet him at the hospital,' Gawn said and pushed her foot down hard on the accelerator.

'What happened to the diamonds?' she asked.

'Nobody came for them. They must have seen us. We took them back.'

Chapter 72

Of course, she couldn't speak to Nina. She couldn't get anywhere near her.

Gawn had found Sharma sitting on his haunches against a wall in a packed A&E reception area. He was surrounded by a roomful of anxious-looking people, some moaning in pain and one retching noisily into a cardboard bowl just beside him. Harassed nurses were gliding in and out while a drunken man harangued one of the receptionists. The woman was safely ensconced behind thick glass which was taking the brunt of his anger as he banged his fist against it and yelled. A uniformed PC arrived and started remonstrating with the drunk. It looked like a scene from some disaster movie, but Gawn knew it was just a typical night in the A&E departments of all the local hospitals.

Sharma saw her and stood up shakily.

'Where is she?' Gawn asked.

'The doctors are examining her now, ma'am.'

'You shouldn't have left her, DC Sharma.'

'She's not going anywhere, ma'am. You didn't see her. She could barely walk when we got to her. She's lost a lot of blood and the triage nurse said she'd need surgery on her breast.'

Sharma was one of the very few who had seen the kidnapper's video message. He had been analysing it, trying to find something in it to help them identify where she was being held.

'I stayed while the nurse was with her,' he said, 'but the doctor asked me to leave. Well, told me to, really. They're taking her down to theatre to clean her wounds. She has a bad infection and she'll need surgery, they think.'

The young officer looked and sounded distressed.

'Did she say anything about where she was held or where Norrie is?'

'She talked about a "Doc". She wasn't making much sense. I don't know whether she meant a doctor. She said Doc had driven off and left her. All she kept asking was where Norrie was. She doesn't know, ma'am.'

Chapter 73

Gawn waited with Sharma in the A&E reception until a petite Filipino nurse appeared and told them Nina had been taken down to theatre. In a tiny voice she explained Nina's condition was stable but she wouldn't be back to a ward for a couple of hours and she advised them to go home and come back later.

Gawn wasn't about to do that, of course, but she was concerned that Sharma was looking very pale, not just tired, but upset, maybe even on the verge of collapse. He was young and relatively inexperienced. She had read his file and knew a little about his past struggles. She didn't want him breaking down so she had taken him along to the canteen. It was open twenty-four hours but at this time of night only vending machine drinks and food were available, but at least there was somewhere to sit and no drunks causing a fuss.

Gawn sat with Sharma, chatting to him about his family, distracting him, until he drank a cup of what the machine had described as tea to which she had added a lot of sugar. He had munched his way through a bar of chocolate she had fetched for him too. When he began to look a little brighter and sounded more like himself, she left him with orders to make sure he was by Nina's bedside as soon as she came out of theatre and to stay there until he was relieved. Someone would be sent to replace him soon, she promised.

As she drove away from the RVH down the Westlink into Belfast, traffic was still light. Her mind was working overtime. They had found Nina. Well, she had found them really. She assumed Maxwell would already have been in touch with his counterpart in Liverpool so Nina's parents would have been informed of the good news. Nina would recover, so they had been told, but she would bear the scars of her experience for the rest of her life. Not just physical scars. Gawn's hand moved to her forehead and she fingered her own scar underneath her hairline.

Pedersen would still be waiting for news. She didn't think Maxwell would have contacted him. He would have left that to her. The perks of rank, she thought to herself grimly.

Back at Castlereagh she made her way to the incident room to catch up on all that had been happening. She hoped there would be some good news waiting for her. She did a doubletake when she saw a woman, whom she thought she recognised, at the far end of the corridor being escorted towards the interview suite sandwiched between Grant and Nolan. She must have made a mistake, she decided, and put it out of her mind.

'Update, Paul,' she barked at the DI as she walked in. She had sounded angrier than she'd intended.

'Sandra found your attackers from the car park.'

He held out a printout to her of an image taken from CCTV. It was just as grainy and useless as she had expected it would be. Two males could just about be made out in the driver and passenger seats but their faces were hidden by ski masks.

'Any joy with the number plate?' she asked, but there was no expectation in her voice.

'Too obscured to be any use.'

'No surprises there then,' she said. 'Have you contacted Liverpool?'

'Aye. I got Starr out of his bed. He was a bit miffed at first but he was alright once I explained he'd be able to give the family some good news. Everybody likes being the bearer of good news, don't they? He's going to get the FLO to arrange travel so Mrs Deeley can come over and see her daughter. She'll be here sometime today. He's to let me know when her plane's due in and we can send a car to pick her up.'

'And what about Pedersen?'

Maxwell looked guilty.

'I thought I would leave that to you, boss. I thought we might have had some good news for him by the time you got back…' he said, his voice trailing off lamely.

Chapter 74

The phone had been answered after only two rings. Gawn knew she should probably have gone to the hotel and spoken to Pedersen in person. She wasn't shying away from facing him. That wasn't her style. But she couldn't take the time.

The ransom had been paid. Nina was safe but what about Norrie? Every second could count in the race to reach him. Maxwell had gathered a search team and they would start looking when the new shift came on duty. She needed to be here.

It was Dahlstrøm's voice she heard answering, even though she had asked to be connected to Pedersen's hotel room.

'Lukas Dahlstrøm,' he announced.

'It's DCI Girvin.'

Gawn heard shuffling and a voice but couldn't make out what was said. Then Pedersen was speaking to her. He must have grabbed the phone from his assistant.

'Have you got him? Is he alright? When can I see him?'

She sucked in her breath. 'We haven't got him yet, sir.'

A strangled cry sounded down the telephone line.

'There's no indication they're going to make any more demands. We'll just have to wait until they let us know where he is. They have no reason to hurt him. You've cooperated. You've done everything they asked.'

'So, we just sit back and wait?' Pedersen asked. He sounded defeated.

'Yes. *You* do. But *we* don't. We're continuing to search and we have some new leads.'

Gawn knew she was stretching the truth, more than a little. Jacob's Island was hardly a lead, but it meant something and she needed to figure out what. If she did, it could lead them to Norrie.

Chapter 75

Gawn sat without moving for what seemed like a long time after her phone call ended. She couldn't get Pedersen's voice out of her head. He had sounded nothing like an urbane diplomat used to dealing with pressurised negotiations. Instead, he had been distraught, asking her how he was going to tell his wife that Norrie was still missing. She had had no answer to give him.

'Get a grip, woman!' she said aloud to herself and ran her fingers through her hair, pushing it back off her face. 'You're not helping anybody feeling sorry for yourself.'

She wasn't giving up yet. Nina was safe in hospital. They had got the diamonds back, although she didn't think Pedersen would care about that. They just needed something to help them find the kidnappers. Maybe Nina would be able to describe her captors or where she had been held; maybe someone would turn up Jacob's Island on an obscure townland map and they could begin to search. Maybe. Maybe. Bloody maybe.

'Boss?'

A sheepish-looking Maxwell had opened her office door without her noticing and was hanging around the frame, watching her. She knew he had made himself scarce when she was ringing the ambassador. He felt guilty about that, no doubt.

'What is it, Paul?'

She kept her voice neutral. She wasn't mad at him. With rank came the hard decisions and the hard jobs.

'You were followed to the graveyard.'

Gawn's eyes widened.

'Are you sure? I didn't see anybody. There was no car behind me.'

'It had its lights turned off.'

'How do you know?' she asked.

'Tower 1 spotted them. It went on after you stopped at the church and emerged onto the old road to Lisburn. A patrol car started following it back towards Belfast. They were going to stop it to breathalyse the driver cos they thought he was probably drunk. But they lost it. It gave them the slip. Deliberately.'

'Why would the kidnappers have been following me? They knew where I was going.'

Gawn remembered thinking that perhaps they'd intended to grab her and hold her hostage too. Had that been the plan? If it was, why hadn't they done it?

Maxwell was still standing there. He hadn't finished yet.

'It was probably some journalist trying to get a story,' Gawn suggested.

'No. Lisburn got a partial number plate from the car and ran it. They've just picked the driver up. Nolan's waiting in the interview suite. I thought she'd be the best one to do the interview.'

Gawn shot him a questioning look.

'Why? You could do it, or Jamie or Jack.'

'Definitely not Jack,' he said. 'It's Jo.'

Chapter 76

Former Detective Constable Josephine Hill, Jo to her friends and ex-colleagues, looked uncomfortable. It had nothing to do with the hard chair on which she was sitting or the slight chill in the room because one of the radiators wasn't working. She would have been in a room like this many, many times before – just sitting on the other side of the table.

Hill had been one of Gawn's team until her last case. Although Professional Standards hadn't been involved and there had been no question of Hill being dismissed or even disciplined, she had decided to resign from the force. Her affair with DC Jack Dee had compromised the investigation and she felt she had let everyone down. Gawn had heard she was a partner in a local firm of private investigators now. She didn't know whether Hill and Dee were still together but Maxwell was right, Dee couldn't question her. And it was better that none of the other officers who had worked alongside Hill did it either.

Sian Nolan walked into the room clutching a notebook to her chest almost like a shield. She glanced up nervously at the camera in the corner of the room. She knew Gawn and Maxwell would be watching the interview. Hill would know it too or at least suspect it. Gawn wondered which of the two was more nervous.

When Nolan started fiddling with her notebook, turning over pages as if she was looking for something, Hill pushed her chair back slightly from the table, scraping it along the tiled floor. It made a screeching noise, setting Gawn's teeth on edge and reminding her of the campervan being lifted out of the water by the tow truck.

'Enough with the bloody games. It's the middle of the night. I'm tired. When is someone going to tell me why I've been dragged out of my bed and brought here?' Hill demanded.

Nolan continued reading, ignoring Hill's question.

'I was driving without lights. So, shoot me, why don't you? I'd got into my car at my friend's house where there were streetlights and I didn't notice I hadn't switched my car headlights on. It hardly warrants the third degree, does it?'

'No one should know better than you, Miss Hill, that the Serious Crime unit does not concern itself with traffic violations,' Nolan said calmly, looking up and holding Hill's angry glare.

'Ms Hill.'

'Ms Hill,' Nolan repeated.

'Then what? Why am I here? Charge me and let me pay my fine or take the points on my licence or whatever you're going to do or tell me what the hell this is about.'

Hill was putting on a show. Gawn knew it. Nolan probably knew it too even though she'd never met Jo Hill before.

'She's not going to cooperate if we treat her like a suspect,' Gawn said to Maxwell. 'It'll only get her back up. She'll tell Sian nothing.'

'She is a suspect. Isn't she?' he asked uncertainly.

'You think Jo's working with the kidnappers? Seriously, Paul? She's involved in some way. Yes. But I can't believe she's gone over to the other side. I'll talk to her myself. In my office. Off the record,' Gawn said and walked out of the room without waiting to let him react.

* * *

'Sit down, Jo,' Gawn said.

The woman didn't move, she just took up a belligerent stance facing her former boss across her desk. There was a time when she would have rushed to obey.

'Please,' Gawn added.

Hill sat down.

'Do you seriously not know why you've been brought here, Jo? You're an intelligent woman. You were following me. You know it and I know it. And I don't have time for any stupid games.'

Gawn watched for a reaction. Hill suddenly seemed to relax. The tension oozed from her body. She exhaled loudly and crossed her legs as if getting comfortable.

. 'I didn't know it was you, boss,' she said and shrugged, unaware that she had subconsciously slipped into calling Gawn 'boss'.

'Seriously?'

'The job was to follow a black Porsche. You've changed your car. Last time I saw you, you were driving a grey Audi. I was just given the registration and details of where I could pick the car up for the tail.'

'From Castlereagh?'

'Yes.'

'You mightn't have known it was me but you knew it was one of us you were following,' Gawn said. 'It had to be a police officer, coming out of here.'

'Serious Crime didn't work out of Castlereagh. Not in my time. I knew it was someone who'd been in the station for some reason, not necessarily a cop. And even cops can get up to some funny business.'

Hill had the grace to look embarrassed. She and Dee had got up to some funny business, hadn't they?

'What were you supposed to do?'

'Just follow you. See where you went. Report back. That's all.'

'Who to?' Gawn asked.

'Client confidentiality. I'm not in the PSNI anymore. When someone comes to us, we promise them complete confidentiality. That, and results of course.'

Hill seemed uneasy again now. She uncrossed her legs and sat up straighter in her chair.

Gawn didn't think Hill had been working for the kidnappers. Apart from the fact that Hill was one of the most hardworking officers she'd known and keen to see criminals behind bars, the kidnappers having her followed wouldn't make any sense.

Gawn was sure someone else had been behind Jo's job. Who it was could be very important. It could lead them to Norrie.

'This is serious, Jo. A girl was missing. Kidnapped. When you were following me, I was on my way to pay the ransom. She's turned up badly hurt now but her boyfriend is still missing. You know all about that sort of situation.'

Hill squirmed on her chair.

'Come on, Jo,' Gawn continued. 'Who wanted me followed? Who's your client? This is important. You could save his life.'

There was a long pause. Too long as far as Gawn was concerned but she didn't try to offer any more arguments. She was letting Hill's conscience do the work for her. Eventually Hill answered.

'I don't know. I wasn't told.'

'Do you often do jobs for people you don't know?'

Gawn was sceptical. The Jo Hill she knew would have wanted to know all the details.

'Our office administrator took the gig. She has the authority to accept straightforward cases so long as we have space on our schedule and we've worked for the client before. And they've paid their bill on time in the past,' Hill added and smiled. 'She was contacted by a solicitor. He uses us all the time.'

'For what?' Gawn asked.

'Matrimonial stuff. Cheating husbands and wives. Evidence in divorce cases especially if there's been a prenup,' Hill said reluctantly. 'It's a lucrative niche market for us.'

'You thought you were following a cheating wife?'

'When I got a proper look and saw who it was, I assumed Sebastian was having you followed.'

'Because I was cheating on him?'

Gawn sounded incredulous and Hill looked embarrassed.

'The solicitor intimated that his client was concerned that his wife was "up to no good". That was how he put it. I was to follow you and see where you went and who you met.'

Was this for real? Was Sebastian having her followed? Gawn believed Hill. She wouldn't make it up. But she couldn't believe Seb thought she was cheating on him. Maybe he was concerned she would put herself in danger.

Either way, she couldn't have him interfering in her work like this.

'Who's the solicitor, Jo?'

'Martin McMurray,' the woman answered reluctantly.

'Martin McMurray of Fraser, Torrens and McMurray?'

'Yes.'

That was no coincidence.

Chapter 77

She was going to have to do it. She couldn't steam into the offices of FTM and accuse them of having her followed. Not if there was any chance it really had been Sebastian who had commissioned them. She was going to have to phone him and ask.

It was only just gone seven but she couldn't put it off. If she hadn't been followed at his instigation, then she needed to know. They could try to pressure the solicitor to find out who had been behind it.

But a tiny voice in the back of her mind was nagging at her and she was finding it hard to silence it. Could it be Sebastian? Was he looking for an excuse for a divorce? They had always joked she was high maintenance. She'd put him through a lot. But he loved her. And their sex life was good. Very good, she'd thought. Why would he want a divorce? Unless he wanted to move back to the US permanently and find someone who could give him a child.

'Gawn. Thank God. You're alright.'

She had expected to hear a sleepy voice but Sebastian was wide awake.

'I was worried sick about you, babe.'

'Why?' she asked.

'You told me you'd be working all night, remember? You wouldn't be home. You're not the only one who can work out clues, you know. I knew the game was afoot, to quote Mr Sherlock Holmes. Then when you hadn't phoned, I wondered if you'd been hurt or something.'

He certainly didn't sound like someone who didn't care about her and was looking to offload her and pick up a newer model. Maybe he'd had her followed to keep her safe? It sounded crazy. Just crazy enough to be the kind of thing he might do.

'Were you having me followed?' she asked. Better to ask straight out.

'Followed? Me?'

He sounded bewildered and aghast. And she knew he wasn't that good an actor. She'd always been able to see right through him when he was being economical with the truth, trying to hide something from her. He couldn't even buy her a surprise present without her realising he was up to something.

'Forget I asked, darling.'

'Is someone following you?' he demanded.

'Not now. No. But there was.'

'And you thought it was something to do with me?'

'They said you were paying them.'

'Give me five minutes alone with them and I'll find out who's really paying them.'

Gawn didn't laugh out loud. She knew that would hurt his feelings but she couldn't help smiling at the image of Sebastian taking on Jo Hill; Hill with her black belt in judo. She'd have him on his back in two seconds.

'Don't worry about it. I'll find out who it was myself. You go back to your writing, darling. I take it that was what you were doing. You sound wide awake.'

'Yes. I've got to a really good bit. So, back to chasing my villain through Jacob's Island, eh?'

She could hear a smile in his voice but she had almost dropped the phone.

'What did you just say?'

'Back to chasing my villain through Jacob's Island. I've started a new book and I'm working on a chapter where my hero is chasing the bad guy through Jacob's Island. You know like you said last night on TV. Like Bill Sykes.'

She didn't know what he was talking about.

'I'm working on something new, Gawn. I have a new main character, a time travelling detective. He's gone back to Victorian London. You gave me the idea mentioning the island in your TV interview.'

'Where's Jacob's Island, Seb?' Gawn asked very quietly and held her breath.

'London. Bermondsey, I think. Somewhere on the river anyway. It was marshland. But it doesn't really exist anymore. It was just a very poor area in Dickens' time. Bill Sykes was chased there in *Oliver Twist* and ended up hanging himself by accident after killing poor Nancy.'

Seb was talking about the characters from a Dickens book as if they were real people he knew well.

'So, it was where the rogues and villains hung out in Victorian London?' she asked.

'Yes.'

This was giving her an idea.

'I've got to go, Seb.'

'Take care, babe. Love ya.'

And she knew he did.

Chapter 78

Gawn was on her way to speak to Maxwell. She saw Rainey coming flying towards her along the corridor brandishing a notebook in her hand almost like a weapon. She looked like some avenging fury.

'I'm in a hurry, Sam. Speak to you later,' Gawn said about to rush past.

'Wait. I found something. Fraser kept notebooks. I've been working my way through them. But I skipped to the 1995 one last night.' Rainey held up the notebook. 'He mentions Jacob's Island in it.'

Gawn stopped suddenly. She swung round.

'Come with me,' she said and took Rainey by the elbow guiding her through the incident room and into Maxwell's office. He looked up in surprise as they rushed in, both looking rather flushed.

'I think I might know what Jacob's Island means. And Sam has found something about it in Fraser's diary as well.'

'What did you find?' Maxwell directed his question to Rainey.

'Fraser mentions Jacob's Island in relation to someone he refers to as Pip. Remember we've come across that name before? One of the text messages asked about Pip. They were looking for him and that made us think of *Great Expectations*.'

'Philip Pirrip,' Maxwell said. 'I remember reading that book in school. I hated it. I thought Pip was a bit of a wimp. But there's always the football manager called Pip too,' he added.

'I don't think they were looking for any football manager, Paul,' Rainey said.

'Philip Pirrip,' Gawn said slowly. 'Yes. That was the character's name. Of course. Philip. Phillips.'

Maxwell's face lit up. 'This Pip is Alan Phillips, you think?'

'Could be. Your shooter wanted to find Pip,' Gawn said to Rainey. 'That's what he asked in the text message to Fraser. And the kidnappers have been trying to get a message to Alan Phillips through abducting his daughter.'

'Jacob's Island seems to be where they met up, Gawn. Fraser doesn't say exactly where it was but the final entry' – Rainey proffered the book to Gawn to read herself – 'says they can never go back there now after the bomb.'

When Gawn raised her head there was a pained look in her eyes.

'Seb said the original Jacob's Island was on marshland. My father and his partner were killed at a nature reserve outside Newtownards. It's marshland. Montgomery told me they were working undercover trying to infiltrate a gang and they'd gone there for a meeting.'

'Could this Jacob's Island be where your father was killed?' she asked.

'Worth a look,' Maxwell said. He was already on his feet and grabbing his jacket from the back of his chair.

'Wait. Hang on, Paul.'

Gawn put her hand on his arm to stop him.

'We don't know what we might be walking into,' she said. 'If we're right and their plan has worked, the kidnappers will be waiting there. Phillips might be there too if he's got the message. If we go charging in, it could turn into a hostage situation or worse, a shoot-out. We need to get hold of a map of the area. And I need to contact Martin McMurray.'

Chapter 79

McMurray had blustered when Gawn had phoned him. She knew he was the weak link. He handled civil litigation for the law firm. He had never dealt with any criminal cases so far as she knew.

She had threatened to come down to his offices with every branch of the PSNI she could think of – Fraud Squad, Child Protection, Organised Crime.

'I'll go through every inch of your work and your life with a fine-tooth comb, Mr McMurray. If you've so much as looked sideways at one of your secretaries or made a false claim on your expenses for extra paper clips, I'll find out and you'll be on the front page of the Sunday papers. I promise you.'

She was bluffing. She knew she couldn't do that and threatening it could backfire on her. He could report her. He probably would and she would be in serious trouble but she wasn't thinking about any of that now.

And her threats were enough.

'There's no need to threaten me, Chief Inspector. I'm always happy to assist the PSNI. I employed Ms Hill's services for a client. All she had to do was follow someone and report back. There was nothing illegal about it.'

'Who?' Gawn demanded.

'He's an old associate of Denton's. They were friends for years.'

Gawn thought she knew the answer but she asked anyway.

'Who?'

'His name's Montgomery. Sir Patrick Montgomery.'

* * *

'Here's the old road and this is the entrance to the Mongash nature reserve,' Gawn said, pointing to a map which Maxwell had pinned up on his office wall.

'According to this local history website' – Maxwell held up a sheaf of pages – 'all the land around this area used to be part of a farm belonging to a family called Jacobs. Old man Jacobs liked bird watching and he built himself a hut in the middle of the marshland. Here's a picture.'

Maxwell pinned up one of the pages.

'This is what it looked like in 1953. It's probably not there anymore. It looks as if it was practically falling down back then.'

'A gang could have been using this back in the day,' Gawn said. 'It would be private, off the beaten track, not the sort of place police would expect.

'It's just a hunch. But it's all we have at the minute. I don't want to involve the ARU. We could end up with egg all over our faces, well I could, if we turn up and there's nothing and no one there except a flock of ducks quacking at us. It's my decision. We'll check it out, quietly, not charge in heavy-handed. Just a small team. You, me and Sam,' she said to Maxwell.

'What about taking Jamie and Sian too?' Maxwell asked. 'Jamie would be useful if we end up in a bit of a fight and Sian's a good shot.'

'I hope we won't be needing to do any shooting. I'm not planning for the O.K. Corral. But, alright,' Gawn said. She didn't remind him she was a good shot too. 'You brief the others, Paul. As quickly as possible. We don't know what's going on or what Montgomery's up to. There's no time to waste.

'Phillips could be at Jacob's Island already. He could be dead already. And God knows where Norrie is.'

Chapter 80

They drove to Newtownards in two unmarked police cars: Maxwell driving one along with Grant and Nolan; Gawn and Rainey in the other. Everyone was wearing body armour.

The ten-mile journey seemed to go on forever. They were keeping to the speed limits and not using blue lights. They didn't want to advertise their approach. Every set of traffic lights they met seemed to be at red. When they turned off the modern dual carriageway onto the old road, it was no better. Now it was the tortuous bends and corners of what had once formed part of the TT race in the late 1920s that slowed them down.

The twenty-minute journey had seemed more like fifty.

Maxwell swung his car into the small lay-by car park for visitors to the nature reserve. Gawn was right behind him, almost on his bumper. There were already two vehicles parked there. One was a small Japanese model and the other a limousine which Gawn recognised.

'Check the number plates,' she ordered Nolan. She turned away quickly. She hadn't been here for over ten years. On that day, she had made herself come to try to slay some of her demons. It hadn't worked.

The sergeant moved away and started typing rapidly onto her tablet.

'You take Sian, when she's finished, and Jamie, and approach from the east. Sam and I'll come from the west,' Gawn told Maxwell. 'That way we should meet anyone in the area. Our first priority is to get any visitors out of the way. We'll meet in the middle which is where the shed should be if it's still standing. Don't approach it, Paul. Just wait.'

Nolan rushed back over to them.

'The car's a rental. The hire company says it was rented out to someone called Pedersen.'

That was not what Gawn had been expecting to hear. Nor had Nolan, if her voice was anything to judge by.

'The other one's a government car. I couldn't get a name for it.'

'We don't need one. I've been in it. It's Montgomery's car,' Gawn said.

'Montgomery *and* Pedersen. What the hell's going on, boss?' Maxwell asked.

'Call for backup,' Gawn ordered Nolan. She didn't care now if it turned out to be a false alarm and she looked foolish. She would risk that. But she didn't think it was much of a risk.

What she wouldn't risk was her team's lives or the lives of any potential hostages. She knew they were dealing with a seriously violent gang. She didn't know what game Montgomery was playing or why Pedersen had appeared in the middle of everything. Perhaps he was trying to negotiate with the kidnappers himself.

Whatever was going on, it couldn't be good.

Chapter 81

Gawn knew they should wait in the car park for backup.

They should wait but they didn't. She couldn't. She was afraid they might already be too late. Members of the public used the reserve to walk their dogs. Someone could arrive at any minute or, although there were no other cars in the car park, could already be here and end up as an innocent victim. Birdwatchers could already be on the marshes. She decided they would move in and set up surveillance and then wait for backup.

They had circled the marshland, Maxwell's team from the east and Gawn and Sam from the west. They met no one nor saw anyone on their way. They had surprised a raft of ducks which had risen into the air noisily, complaining loudly at their habitat being disturbed. Gawn hoped that hadn't alerted anyone to their approach.

'There it is, boss,' Maxwell whispered, keeping his voice low just in case there was someone inside the ramshackle building.

The five were huddled behind a clump of tall grasses shielding them from the wooden structure which looked as if it was about to collapse. The one window was boarded up and the roof had gaping holes in it. The door was lying open. It would make a great spot for a children's den and, thirty years ago, it would have made a good site for secret meetings planning robberies or whatever crime was next on the Tates' agenda.

'Jamie, see how close you can get without being seen. We need to know if anyone's inside,' Gawn ordered. 'And take care. I don't want any heroes.'

They watched as Grant zigzagged his way across the piece of ground moving from bush to bush until he reached the building. He flattened himself against the outer wall and they saw him craning his neck forward for just an instant to try to get a view inside. He turned back to them and held up his hand to stop them moving forward. They watched again as he made his way back to them.

Grant's eyes were bright with excitement and his voice was breathy.

'There are people inside alright. I could hear them talking.'

'How many?' Maxwell asked.

'Not sure, sir. At least three. I caught a glimpse of Phillips and a great big man with a beard.'

'That's Montgomery,' Gawn said. 'What were they doing?' she asked.

'A man with his back to me was doing all the talking. The other two were on their knees. And the man was walking up and down in front of them. He kept on and on about being shafted; about them being the reason his brother is dead. He has a gun,' Grant said.

'Where's Pedersen?' Maxwell asked.

'Wrong question, officer.'

Chapter 82

The voice had come out of nowhere. They all swung around and looked behind them, to see a smiling Lukas Dahlstrøm with a gun in his hand pointed at them.

'Don't try anything, please. Tell them, Chief Inspector. I'm not joking. I know five to one is quite good odds for you, but I'd take a few of you out before you managed to get to me. Perhaps even ladies first?' He smiled again, his eyes moving along the line of three women. It was a cold calculating smile.

He sounded reasonable – as if he was discussing some business venture rather than the shooting of police officers. But Gawn knew he was deadly serious. She had miscalculated with him. He had seemed charming and devoted to the Pedersen family, even offering to deliver the ransom himself. She had overlooked him. They hadn't done a background check on him, just accepted him at face value. Now her mistake was coming back to bite them.

'Do what he says,' Gawn ordered.

'Take your weapons, one by one, very carefully, and lay them on the ground in front of you. No nonsense, please. Then take a step back from them.'

'Do it,' Gawn ordered and nodded her head.

One by one, they complied, Maxwell first. When Grant lifted his gun, he paused. Gawn could see the calculation cross his mind.

'Put your weapon down now, DC Grant,' she said sharply.

Gawn was last to take her gun slowly from its holster and set it on the muddy ground in front of her. She had considered taking a shot at Dahlstrøm. She knew she could hit him at this range but maybe not before he could get a shot off and one of the others could be injured or killed. She couldn't risk it. Backup was on its way. They just needed to keep calm and wait.

She straightened up. 'What now, Dahlstrøm?'

'Now, we go inside for a nice chat. No shenanigans, Chief Inspector,' he said and smiled at her.

In a line, like a school party out for a nature visit, the five walked in front of Dahlstrøm towards the open door.

'Go on,' the Norwegian ordered. 'Inside.'

Inside the shed it was dark and shadowy and there was the odour of dead animals and human excrement. Montgomery and Phillips looked up expectantly when Maxwell led the little troupe into the room. Perhaps they anticipated rescue. The man at the front had a gun trained on them. He spun round and leered at the sight of the newcomers and then smiled as he recognised Gawn.

'Brought you a present, Madas,' Dahlstrøm said. 'They were outside. You were lucky I needed to get the cable ties from my car or they'd have surprised you.'

Madas Tate strutted along the line of police officers until he came face to face with Gawn. She was surprised when she saw him close up. He was an old man. His chin was covered in grey stubble and his eyes had that weak look she associated with the elderly.

'Chief Inspector Girvin, we meet again.'

Gawn could have laughed in his face. It was like a line from some corny fifties film. But she recognised the raspy voice she had heard in the car park and knew he was deadly serious.

'I knew your father,' he said. 'He died here, you know.' Tate swung the gun around taking in the whole room. 'But of course you know. It'll be a closing of the circle for you to die here too.'

Tate laughed. It was a chilling sound.

Gawn didn't look at the others. She just hoped no one would try to play the hero. Backup was on its way. They should be with them soon. It was just a matter of playing for time.

'Tie them up,' Tate ordered the Norwegian. When Dahlstrøm looked around helplessly, Tate yelled, 'The cable ties, you fool. And tie these two as well.' He gestured to Montgomery and Phillips who were kneeling in front of him with their hands on their heads.

One by one, the five had their hands secured behind their backs and were made to kneel on the floor in front of Tate. He watched carefully, never moving his gun from them. A drool of saliva escaped the side of his mouth. He was enjoying himself. He wiped it away with the back of his hand.

Tate moved across then to Montgomery and Phillips. He had his back to Gawn and the others now. They heard the noise as a zip was pulled down and watched as a stream of urine hit the two men in their faces. Tate was laughing. Gawn glimpsed Montgomery's face. His jaw was clenched. He was furious. Phillips' eyes were tight closed. Tate's maniacal laughing reminded Gawn of her last case. She dug her fingernails into the palms of her hands in helplessness.

Tate zipped himself back up and the laughter died on his lips. He turned around again.

'That's what I think of them,' he said with a sneer.

Dahlstrøm was moving across to Montgomery and Phillips to tie them up too, but stopped. 'Now,' he said, 'we just have our business to finish, Madas, and then I'll leave you to do whatever you want to these ones.' He nodded at the two men. 'I want no part of it. Killing wasn't part of our arrangement. Just the kidnapping.'

When Tate didn't respond, seeming not even to have heard him, Dahlstrøm shouted, 'The diamonds. I'm here to get them, remember? Where are they?'

It almost looked as if Tate didn't know what the Norwegian was talking about; as if he had forgotten completely about any ransom.

'The diamonds,' Tate repeated and tapped his forehead with the muzzle of his gun as if he was trying to remember. 'Ah yes, the diamonds. Of course. I'm afraid they're gone, Lukas. Little Nina took them. Pedersen will get them back, I guess. Fair exchange for his son. He won't get him back.' He laughed. 'The diamonds mean nothing to me. They never did. I only wanted my revenge. On these two. And this one is a bonus. I never expected her to turn up here as well,' he added, swinging round and looking at Gawn where she knelt in front of him. 'Denton's gone and these three will be joining him in hell.'

His voice suddenly softened. It was almost as if he had forgotten anyone else was there with him. He was talking to himself or some unseen person from his memory.

'Poor wee Niall,' he said. 'He was autistic, you know. That's what they call it these days. "Wanting" was what they used to call it. My ma always said he had "a wee want" and I was to look after him. He died in that hell hole of a prison. He didn't deserve that.' His voice had hardened again. He was shouting.

Gawn wanted to keep him talking. That was their best chance. Once he stopped, he would start killing.

'Niall was your brother?' she asked.

'Yes. My poor wee brother. A kind, gentle wee soul. Wouldn't have hurt a fly. He went everywhere with me but he didn't know what was going on half the time. He lived in his own wee world. He didn't understand what we were doing. I told them that.'

Tate gestured again towards the two kneeling men waving his gun at them.

'I said he had nothing to do with anything. He didn't know anything. He'd never done anything. I told them. I told Denton too. He promised he'd get Niall off. He lied to me. And that bastard named him just because the kid had been with me when he brought us the bits for the bomb,' he said, pointing to Phillips. 'They didn't even put us in the same prison. I was transferred and he was left without me to protect him. He hanged himself, they said. I never even got to see him or go to his funeral. Bastards!'

He flung the word at Montgomery and Phillips, spittle flying out his mouth.

Tate was crying now and rocking backwards and forwards on his heels. Gawn realised he was becoming more unstable. He could do anything at any time. He was past any reasoning stage.

'You promised me the diamonds, you lying bastard. That was our deal,' Dahlstrøm shouted.

He made a sudden charge towards Tate as if he was going to grab him by the arm. Without a moment's hesitation, Tate fired his gun at almost point-blank range and the Norwegian fell against him. Tate moved back, allowing Dahlstrøm's body to fall to the ground. The Norwegian made no sound as his face hit the floor, but a puff of dust rose into the air. He was already dead, a bloody red circle on the centre of his chest.

'As for you two,' Tate said, turning to look at Phillips and Montgomery, 'once I deal with you and this bitch' – his look switched to Gawn – 'I'll light a nice wee bonfire. This place will go up like a fuckin' matchstick. It'll be like the twelfth of July. It'll take them weeks to identify all the bodies and work out who's who.'

Gawn couldn't just stand by and watch two men being executed in cold blood or the prospect of her team being incinerated. There was madness in Tate's eyes.

Tate raised his gun slowly towards Phillips, savouring his moment of revenge. Gawn watched as Phillips closed his eyes again, anticipating his imminent death. He was shaking uncontrollably, in danger of falling over. His lips began to move in a silent prayer.

Gawn had been watching Montgomery. Their eyes had met and he had blinked and moved his head. Just a fraction but she knew he was going to try something. He wasn't the kind of man who would just wait there and let himself and Phillips be shot.

She propelled herself forward from her kneeling position and rammed Tate at the back of his knees with her shoulder. He doubled up and lost hold of his gun in surprise. He fell forward into Montgomery's arms. The Englishman sprang into action with an unexpected speed for someone his age and size. He began struggling with the thug, lifting him up off his feet.

Montgomery was a big man, and strong. He might look soft and flabby, well-suited behind a desk, but he hadn't forgotten his army training. He slammed his fist into Tate's stomach, bending him double, and followed up with an uppercut to his jaw as good as any Mancarelli might have scored in his boxing days. Tate was unconscious before he reached the ground.

Montgomery released Gawn, cutting her cable ties with a Swiss army penknife he had produced from his pocket. How appropriate and how typical of the man to carry one of those, Gawn thought – straight out of some schoolboy's adventure comic. He freed her first and helped her to her feet.

They heard their backup arriving. There were warning shouts and suddenly the room was filled with armed men and women. They began releasing the others. Paramedics appeared and checked on Dahlstrøm and Tate.

Montgomery drew Gawn outside.

'I didn't expect you to be saving me,' Montgomery said.

'I could say the same thing, Sir Patrick,' Gawn replied.

'Then I suppose you could say we're even. I always felt I'd got your father killed, you know. I'm glad I got the chance to even the scales.'

He saw the look on her face and hurried on.

'I'm not some monster, Gawn, and I wasn't back then either. Sometimes we had to do things we wouldn't have even contemplated under different circumstances. You were a soldier. You know what it's like. You do what you have to do.

'And I didn't get your father killed. He knew what he was taking on. He'd volunteered. He and Dalton both did. It was just pure bad luck. Some petty criminal recognised Dalton and made them both for police officers. He sold the information to Tate.' He looked back at the handcuffed figure being led away by an excited-looking Grant and a rather more pale-faced Nolan. 'For the price of a fix. That's how much their lives were worth.'

'You were behind all this weren't you? It was you who wanted me in charge and you had me followed when I was delivering the ransom.'

'Yes. As soon as Pedersen contacted me about the kidnapping I had a good idea it was all about Alan Phillips. But I didn't know where he was to warn him and I didn't know which of the gangs might be looking for him. I couldn't even trust the PSNI fully. Some of them might still have connections. I needed someone I could trust.'

'Me?' Gawn asked in a small voice.

He nodded.

'That's why you had Jo follow me? You didn't know where I was going.'

'Jo?' Montgomery looked puzzled.

'It doesn't matter now. Nina's safe and so is her father. I'm not so sure Norrie will have been so lucky.'

'Just like your father, you didn't let me down, Gawn. He would be proud of you.'

He held out his hand. After a moment's hesitation, she took it.

Chapter 83

'You'll fly to Oslo next week and represent the PSNI at Norbert Pedersen's funeral.'

Gawn knew Wilkinson was not asking. She was telling. Gawn usually tried to avoid funerals but this time she was glad she was going to have the opportunity to tell Ambassador Pedersen in person how sorry she was for his loss.

She felt no responsibility for Norrie's death. Jenny Norris had carried out the post-mortem on the Norwegian's body after it had been recovered weighted down in the reservoir. The pathologist had been able to reassure her that the man was already dead before she had even been assigned to the case. There was nothing she could have done to save him. He'd tried to bargain with the kidnappers to save himself and Nina but he'd been discarded as of no use to Tate once he had given up his passwords and shown the gang how to upload his vlogs.

Dahlstrøm's funeral would be a smaller affair and no one from the PSNI would be attending. The idea for the kidnap and ransom had been his, according to Tate. And Dahlstrøm wasn't around to contradict him.

Tate had been happy to tell everyone all about what he had done. He was proud of it. He had spent nearly thirty years thinking Phillips was dead until one day he had glimpsed the photograph of the man in Nina and Norrie's vlog. It was pure bad luck for Phillips. It wasn't the sort of thing Tate ever watched but some of his younger cronies had been watching it on their phones and showed the couple to him, laughing over the busty woman and making lewd comments. Tate had recognised the man who he believed had betrayed him and killed his brother.

Tate had flown to Oslo to try to find out more about Nina, thinking her father might be living there with her. Jack Dee had confirmed the trip from the airline's records. But Tate had met up with Dahlstrøm instead of Nina. The Norwegian had provided him with information about the two vloggers and suggested that, instead of just grabbing the girl and torturing her to find her father's whereabouts, he should kidnap the pair. The idea of demanding diamonds had been his as well. He'd been promised the diamonds as his pay-off.

Now Tate was under psychiatric assessment. He might never be deemed fit to stand trial. That would be down to the experts. Either way, he would never be out of an institution again. They had seven witnesses to his murder of Dahlstrøm. He couldn't deny it. Not that he even wanted to, it seemed.

He'd named Gary Napier, known to everyone as Sniffy because of his problem with allergies, as Fraser's shooter and one of the kidnappers. Napier had no criminal record and wasn't on the PSNI database but they had caught up with him quickly once they knew who they were looking for. DNA found on Fraser's body where Napier had spat on him, had come back to confirm his presence at the crime scene. Rainey's first big case as SIO had ended with an arrest, and a conviction should follow.

They hadn't found Charlie Saxsby yet, but it was only a matter of time. He had been the other kidnapper, the other man from the multi-storey car park. Nina had told them 'Doc', as she called him, had saved her from Sneezy – or Sniffy – when he had been going to slice her up. He had convinced the man he would take care of her and had then driven her to a field near the graveyard. He had left her there and told her to go to the grave. He knew it would be watched and she would be taken to hospital.

'Don't feel too bad about Norrie Pedersen, Gawn. You did your best. The chief constable is delighted with the outcome. And Sir Patrick was very quick to point out to him that he had insisted on you being put in charge of the case. Sir Patrick is a man who likes to be right. He made the correct judgement about you, he says,' Wilkinson told her.

Gawn still wasn't sure whether she had made the correct judgement about him. She just hoped their paths would never cross again.

List of characters

DCI Gawn Girvin
Sebastian Girvin-York – Gawn's husband
Sir Patrick Montgomery – Department for Business and Trade
Chief Constable Nigel Huntingdon
Assistant Chief Constable Anne Wilkinson – Crime Department
Chief Superintendent Ronnie Clark – Special Operations
Superintendent Harry Floyd – Intelligence Branch
Jorgen Pedersen – Norwegian Ambassador
Nina & Norrie – vloggers
Superintendent Matt Lynch – Metropolitan Police
DI Paul Maxwell
Kerri Maxwell – Maxwell's wife
DC Jamie Grant
DC John 'Jack' Dee
Dr Jenny Norris – pathologist
DS Sian Nolan
DC Sandra Watt
DC Rohan Sharma
Lukas Dahlstrøm – PA to Norwegian Ambassador
Diane – barista
Denton Fraser – solicitor
DI Sam Rainey
Aoife McWilliams – Strategic Communications and Engagement
Inspector Busch – Kripos
Mrs Ritchie – Fraser's housekeeper
Mark Ferguson – crime scene manager
Norman Nabney & Keith Nelson – fishermen

DI Starr– Merseyside Police
DC Ingram – FLO
Madas Tate
Niall Tate – Madas's brother
Barry Hunter & Sarah Mullvenny – TV presenters
Myra & Julie– TV crew
Gerald Deeley
Marie Deeley
Gary Napier
Charlie Saxsby
Joey Mancarelli
Alan Phillips

If you enjoyed this book, please let others know by leaving a quick review on Amazon. Also, if you spot anything untoward in the paperback, get in touch. We strive for the best quality and appreciate reader feedback.

editor@thebookfolks.com

MORE IN THIS SERIES

*All FREE with Kindle Unlimited and available in paperback.
Books 1 and 2 are now also available as audiobooks.*

THE PERFUME KILLER (Book 1)

Stumped in a multiple murder investigation, with the only
clue being a perfume bottle top left at a crime scene,
DCI Gawn Girvin must wait for a serial killer to make a
wrong move. Unless she puts herself in the firing line.

MURDER SKY HIGH (Book 2)

When a plane passenger fails to reach his destination alive,
Belfast police detective Gawn Girvin is tasked with
understanding how he died. But determining who killed him
begs the bigger question of why, and answering this leads
the police to a dangerous encounter with a deadly foe.

A FORCE TO BE RECKONED WITH (Book 3)

Investigating a cold case about a missing person, DCI Gawn Girvin stumbles upon another unsolved crime. A murder. But that is just the start of her problems. The clues point to powerful people who will stop at nothing to protect themselves, and some look like they're dangerously close to home.

KILLING THE VIBE (Book 4)

After a man's body is found with strange markings on his back, DCI Girvin and her team try to establish his identity. Convinced they are dealing with a personally motivated crime, the trail leads them to a group of people involved in a pop band during their youth. Will the killer face the music or get off scot-free?

THAT MUCH SHE KNEW (Book 5)

A woman is found murdered. The same night, the office pathologist Jenny Norris goes missing. Worried that her colleague might be implicated, DCI Gawn Girvin in secret investigates the connection between the women. But Jenny has left few clues to go on, and before long Girvin's solo tactics risk muddling the murder investigation and putting her in danger.

MURDER ON THE TABLE (Book 6)

A charity dinner event should be a light-hearted affair, but two people dying as the result of one is certainly likely to put a damper on proceedings. DCI Gawn Girvin is actually an attendee, and ready at the scene to help establish if murder was on the table. But the bigger question is why, and if Gawn can catch a wily killer.

NOTHING BUT SMILES (Book 7)

A serial stalker is terrorising women on the streets of Belfast. The victims wake up with no recollection of the night before, but with a smiley-face calling card daubed on their bodies. DCI Gawn Girvin takes on the case although before long she herself is targeted. She must catch the sick creep before matters escalate.

OTHER TITLES OF INTEREST

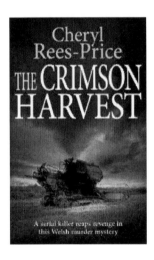

THE CRIMSON HARVEST by Cheryl Rees-Price

Unflappable cop DI Winter Meadows has his wedding
plans interrupted when bodies begin to turn up on his
patch. The Welsh police have a serial killer on their hands
and no stone is left unturned in the hunt. But only a
detective who truly understands the community will be
able to catch a killer in their midst.

Available free with Kindle Unlimited and in paperback!

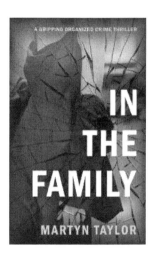

IN THE FAMILY by Martyn Taylor

When a former gangland boss is found shot dead, the investigation will take DI Penelope Darling into the nether regions of her city's criminal world. But finding the killer will require keeping her eyes open to the unexpected. She'll need to have her wits about her to stop a ruthless individual from getting away with murder.

Available free with Kindle Unlimited and in paperback!

Printed by Amazon Italia Logistica S.r.l.
Torrazza Piemonte (TO), Italy

62639050R00134